The Secret of Walla Wunga Forest

Joe Shandrowski

Huga Tuga Creations LLC
Reading Rocks!

Huga Tuga Creations LLC
76 Beacon View Drive
Fairfield, CT 06825
www.hugatuga.com

Story by: Joe Shandrowski
Cover design by Joe Shandrowski
Cover illustration by Jose Ramos

Published by Huga Tuga Creations LLC
www.hugatuga.com

Date of production: November 2015
First edition copy

Printed and bound in the United States of America

*

Dedicated to:
Skylar, James, Danika,
Jessamyn, Raymond
Matthew & Katie

*

CHAPTER 1
The Wind Dragon

It wasn't your typical summer day in Walla Wunga Forest. Usually the animals would be wandering around, playing in the trees, having a snack or enjoying a nap. This day, however, they were scurrying about with panic in their step. There was good reason for them to be spooked: Word had spread across the forest that a wicked storm was on its way, the likes of which the forest had not seen in one hundred years. In fact, today marked the anniversary of that first storm.

Scientists believe animals are born with a sixth sense that allows them to foresee dangerous weather. Nevertheless, the animals of Walla Wunga Forest depended upon a more feathery approach to forecasting. Their method was a "hoot," some would say: They received their daily weather from a grumpy old owl named Wetherbee. Simply put, the grumpier he was, the worse the weather would be.

Yesterday, at the crack of dawn, he had stepped onto the ledge of his tree trunk, let out a simple grunt, and stepped back inside. Except for a few clouds, it turned out to be a beautiful day.

Today, however, was a far different story. From the second his eyes popped open, Wetherbee was on the grump. "Stop running up and down my tree, you nut-headed squirrels!" He yelled as he swatted away a butterfly. "OUCH!" He followed with a shout. "You made me throw my back out."

The grumpiness didn't end there. He complained about buzzing bees, his wobbling knees, and a bad case of gas that could peel the bark off a tree.

It was Wetherbee's great-great-grandfather, Mortimer, who had predicted the last storm that occurred one hundred years ago. "I have a bad feeling about this," Ricky the Raccoon said. Ricky lived in a hollowed-out oak tree next door to Wetherbee the Owl.

Just hours after Mortimer had made his weather prediction one hundred years ago, the beautiful morning skies had turned pitch black, as if it were the dead of night. Out of the dark and menacing clouds appeared a funnel of wind as powerful as a thousand tornadoes. In the funnel was a red-eyed Wind Dragon, fire dripping from its razor-sharp fangs, wings charged with bolts of lightning, a serpent's tail and skin so thin you could see right through to its rotting bones.

The Wind Dragon had twisted through the forest with lightning speed and destroyed everything in its path. Even the 200-year-old oak trees didn't stand a chance against its powerful force. They were ripped from their roots as if they were mere twigs, tossed high into the air, and swallowed up by the black clouds.

When the storm had ended, a chipmunk popped his head out of a hole and summed up what he saw: "Yikity Yikes."

With the land in ruins, the animals had packed up their belongings and made the long journey to the other side of Mount Chubaluba. They knew they could never go home again. And there was a good reason why.

Today, a hundred years after the Wind Dragon rocked the forest, not a single tree, flower, or blade of grass has ever grown back. In fact, the land remains shadowed in a dark and eerie mist.

The animals call it Samp Mortar Swamp, home to the creepiest and most evil creatures of the forest, including trees with claw-like branches and mutated insects ten times their normal size. No animal has ever gone near, let alone stepped into the swamp, out of fear they would simply vanish into the ghostly mist.

To show their defiance, the animals of Walla Wunga Forest gave the Wind Dragon a nickname, Bubbles. It was their way of showing the Wind Dragon they weren't intimidated by its wrath. Rumor had it the Wind Dragon didn't take too kindly to the name: It vowed to return and seek its revenge or, in its own words, "Silence the forest forevermore."

Since today was the one-hundredth anniversary of its last visit, and Wetherbee was grumping like there was no tomorrow, the animals feared the Wind Dragon was about to rise again.

"Where is my coffee mug? Yuck! I think I just swallowed a bug." Wetherbee's whining was nonstop.

"I think you're right," said Ricky's best friend, Shelby the Squirrel. "This is going to be really, really bad."

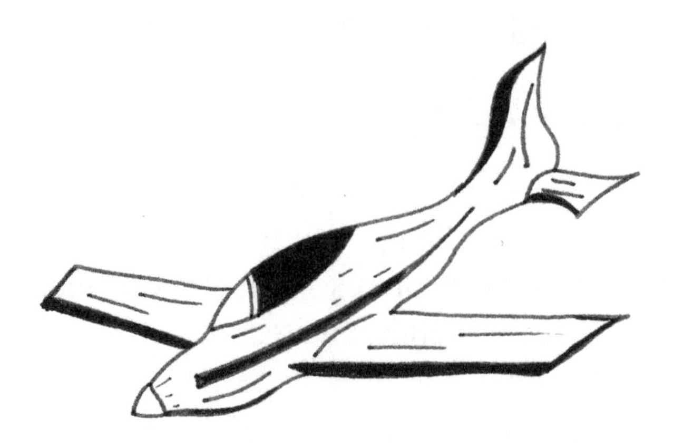

CHAPTER 2
The Rescue

As Wetherbee predicted, the edge of the storm quickly consumed the skies over Walla Wunga Forest. Only a patch of the blue sky remained. The animals picked up their pace, figuring the Wind Dragon could not be far behind.

"We'd better hurry," said Ricky the Raccoon.

"Cripes! You can say that again," said his Grandpa Paulie.

"There's no telling what the Wind Dragon has planned."

"What's all that scurrying about? You're giving me a headache," Wetherbee said with a typical snarl.

"Sorry, Mr. Owl. We'll try to be quieter," Ricky replied.

"Don't waste your time with Mr. Sunshine," Grandpa Paulie snapped back.

At that moment, the animals stopped what they were doing and looked up. A very familiar sound echoed across the sky. It was Ranger Mike Crawford's airplane. Like clockwork, Ranger Mike flew over the forest twice a day to make sure all remained calm and quiet.

Mike was the Walla Wunga Forest head ranger, but in the eyes of the animals he was a superhero. It was his job to protect the forest and all its many creatures, and he took his job very seriously.

The animals watched for a little while and then continued on with the task of securing their homes. A few minutes later they heard another noise. This noise was not familiar.

Ranger Mike's airplane began to flutter and sputter overhead.

"Oh no!" Said Shelby as she stepped alongside Ricky. "Something is wrong, Ricky."

"I'm afraid you're right, Shelby," Ricky replied.

A bright light then flashed from the front of the plane, and the engine shut down.

Shelby, Ricky and all the other animals watched in horror as the plane twirled from the sky and disappeared over the mountainside, leaving behind only a trail of smoke. A faint "thump" could be heard in the distance.

Just then, out of the smoke appeared a mysterious object flopping in the wind. It was falling fast and heading right toward the oldest oak tree in the forest – 3,455 years old to be exact – known as the Mighty Moses.

"What is that?" Asked Shelby's little sister, Katina, as she squinted to get a better look.

"I don't know," Shelby replied. "I can barely tell through all the smoke, but it looks a lot like a giant picnic blanket."

"Hmmm . . . kinda," Ricky said. "I remember seeing something like it before."

The closer the object fell to earth, the more nervous the animals became. Not knowing what the object was made them all jittery. To be safe, they quickly took cover.

While hiding behind a tree stump, Ricky remembered where he had seen the unusual object. "Wait! That's it!" Ricky said.

He scampered to his bedroom and over to an old weather-beaten book he'd found at a burnt-out campsite many years before. The book was so bulky it took his father, grandfather, and three brothers to carry it from the campsite up into his bedroom.

Ricky quickly swept away the leaves that covered the book. The word ENCYCLOPEDIA was written across the top in faded black letters. An encyclopedia was a book of knowledge used by humans to find information on everything from presidents to pirates to space aliens to dinosaurs.

"It's in here somewhere; I just know it," he said as he yanked open the cover and quickly flipped through the pages. "Yes. Found it. A parachute. A rescue device that slows one's fall from the sky." Ricky looked up. "Oh no! Ranger Mike must be underneath! We have to help – and fast!"

What made Ricky nervous was the fact that the parachute was not falling slowly, and it wasn't puffy like the one in the book; it was all tangled up.

Ricky scooted from his bedroom, but it was too late. The parachute had landed over a sinkhole right alongside the Mighty Moses.

One by one, the animals came out of hiding and gathered around the mysterious object. Ricky quickly explained to the animals what it was.

"I'm afraid Ranger Mike is underneath the parachute," he said. The animals did not hesitate. They each grabbed an edge of the parachute and lifted it away.

Ricky was right. Ranger Mike was indeed under the parachute, and pretty banged up. His face was all red, his right leg was twisted, and he had a big old lump on his head. He tried to speak, but the pain was so severe all he could do was moan and groan.

"Pssst . . . everybody, follow me," whispered Ricky.

The animals backed away gently and huddled a short distance from the hole.

"Ranger Mike is hurt really badly and in need of our help," Ricky said.

"You're right, Ricky," a beaver named Bart agreed, "but what can we do?"

"Well, we have to do something," Ricky said as the faint sound of thunder was heard in the distance. "We can't leave him here!"

"Yeah, Ricky's right. If we don't help him, he will never make it through the night! The Wind Dragon will get him for sure!" Shelby said.

Suddenly, a loud menacing growl echoed across the forest. The animals cringed and slowly turned toward Mount Chubaluba. Was it the Wind Dragon? Some would say it was worse.

Prowling on the edge of his lair, some 200 feet up the mountainside, appeared the most feared animal in Walla Wunga Forest: a mountain lion named Tombstone.

"This is bad with a capital B," Ricky said with a lump in his throat. He had good reason to be concerned.

There was nothing more horrifying to the animals in Walla Wunga Forest than the thought of Tombstone's bloodstained fangs flashing before their eyes.

Any unlucky fool that ventured into Tombstone's path would fall victim to his hungry belly. "An invitation to dinner," Tombstone would say, "my dinner."

"Sorry, but I'm outta here," said Mongo the Muskrat. "Me too," said Lola the Lizard. "Me three," everyone else agreed.

"I hate to say it, but they're right," said Bart. "The risk is too great. We have our families to think about."

All the animals turned to leave.

"No, wait! We can't run and hide! Come on, guys, this is Ranger Mike," Ricky pleaded, "He has spent his whole life making sure the forest stays clean and free so we can have fresh air to breathe and pure water to drink. It's time we pay him back for all the good he's done. We're his only hope, guys. And besides, we made a promise."

The animals stopped dead in their tracks.

"Ricky is right. We made a promise," Shelby said.

"What promise is that?" Asked Julia the Mouse.

"How old are you, Julia?" Shelby asked.

"I'm one month old," she replied.

"You see, Julia," Shelby said as all the young animals gathered around to listen, "many, many years ago, a massive fire spread across Walla Wunga Forest. The fire destroyed much of the forest, including Walla Wunga Castle."

"Wow! There was a castle?" Julia asked. "Where?" The youngsters spun their heads in all directions.

"Well, that remains a mystery. Some say it stood at the very top of Mount Chubaluba. Others say it was right here where we are standing."

"What did the castle look like?"

"It was a magical place. The castle stood as high as the eye could see. It was made of diamonds and pearls with a beautiful rainbow passing over its peak. The rainbow was home to a blessing of unicorns."

"Unicorns? That is so awesome!" Said Julia.

"Yes, it was." Shelby said. "However, the magic didn't end there. The lawn in front of the castle was just as enchanting. It was lined with the brightest and most colorful flowers you could ever imagine, and there were giant palm trees swaying in the breeze. But most amazing of all was a magnificent waterfall made of silver and gold."

"Wow!" Said the youngsters.

"Double wow!" Bart the Beaver agreed. He was just as mesmerized by Shelby's words as the youngsters were.

"What made Walla Wunga Castle even more special was the fact that the gates to the castle were never closed. Animals and humans were free to roam, as if the castle with all its splendor were their very own."

"Who lived in the castle? Was it a princess?"

Shelby smiled. "Actually, the castle was home to a Woodland Spirit named Nia. After the fire, Nia vowed to protect us animals and humans and do everything she could to make sure a disaster like that would never happen again."

"Truly a tale of wonder," said Merlin the Owl as he floated over to Shelby and landed on a boulder bulging from the ground.

Merlin lived in a tree trunk across the dirt path from Wetherbee. Unlike Wetherbee, everyone loved Merlin. He was considered the "grandpa" of Walla Wunga Forest. If you had a problem, he always had a few words of wisdom to make you feel better. In fact, have you heard of the saying "wise old owl"? It was created because of Merlin.

"But make no mistake, my children," Merlin continued. "This tale isn't a legend or a dream; it is as true as the day is long. Nia was very real. And like Ranger Mike is to all of us today, Nia was a hero in the eyes of your great-great-great-great-grandfathers.

Her spirit has remained within the boundaries of Walla Wunga Forest ever since.

"Sometimes she would appear to us, in our time of need, on the wings of a soft summer breeze. All she ever asked in return was for us animals to make a simple promise: that we would take care of the forest and, most importantly, take care of one another as if we are all family."

Shelby looked into the faces of all the animals that had gathered around. "Ranger Mike may not have fur or whiskers or four paws, but he is part of our family. If we walk away, we'll not only break our promise to Nia, but we'll break his heart."

The animals looked at one another and shook their heads in agreement. Though it might cost them in the end, they all knew Shelby was right. They couldn't turn their backs on Ranger Mike.

"Well, does anyone have an idea?" Asked Satch the Copperhead Snake.

Everyone went silent. No one had a clue.

"I know," Ricky said, stepping forward. "We can ask Ranger Mike to write a note, and we can race to the Ranger Station to get help."

"Wait a minute, Ricky, are you nuts?" Said Bart's twin brother Barry the Beaver. "That would mean we would have to break the forest animals' Code of Silence. If the humans knew that we could speak, do you know what they would do?"

"No, what?" Asked a rabbit named Clyde.

"They would round us up and put us in a zoo," Barry answered.

"A zoo? What's that?" Asked Mongo the Muskrat.

"It's not a pretty place, I'll tell you that," Bart said. "The humans lock you up behind these iron bars, and they stare and take pictures as if you were some sort of a two-headed monster from Mars."

"Yeah, and speaking of nuts," Waldo the Weasel said, "little kids stroll by and throw peanuts at your head as if you're some kind of furry bull's-eye."

"Well, unless someone else has an idea, I think we have no choice. We can trust Ranger Mike with our secret. I know we can!" Ricky exclaimed.

All the animals mumbled in agreement. They stepped back over to the hole and looked down. "Hello there," Ricky said. Ranger Mike slowly lifted his head. He expected to see another ranger, and boy, was he surprised when he saw this pack of furry creatures staring back at him with their beady little eyes!

"Wow, I must have whacked my head something awful," he said to himself, rubbing his hand gently over the bump. "That must be it, sure, I'm seeing and hearing things."

He blinked five times, shook his head, and looked up again. He expected the vision to disappear, but instead things turned even odder. The animals had smiles on their faces, and they were waving at him.

He tried to get up by using a root from the Mighty Moses as a crutch, but the pain in his leg was too great. "Ouch!" He screamed and fell back down.

"You better just lie there and try to rest," Shelby said.

"This is crazy! You're animals and animals can't talk," he replied.

"Don't worry about that now," Ricky said. "You just stay put and we'll go get some help."

"But how?" Ranger Mike asked. "Wait a minute – my cell phone. I can use my cell phone to call for help." He patted down his pockets, but it was nowhere to be found. "It must have fallen out when I jumped from the plane."

Ranger Mike looked at the animals. They were staring back at him, puzzled. He could tell they had no idea what he was talking about.

"Sorry. A cell phone," he explained, "is a small, rectangular gadget that lights up. You can talk to someone on the other side of the forest."

"Oh, okay. We will try our best to find it," Ricky said. "In the meantime, we thought you could write a note explaining where you are, and we would race through the forest to the Ranger Station. We would do it," Ricky said as he raised his paw, "but as you can see, we have no thumbs."

"I don't have anything to write with. The plane engine lit on fire. I dumped out the remaining gasoline so the plane wouldn't explode when it crashed and then bailed out. I simply didn't have time to retrieve my survival kit," Ranger Mike replied.

"No problem at all," said Bart the Beaver. "One writing tool coming up!"

Walla Wunga Forest, like many forests, was rich in minerals, including copper, silver, gold, and, most important of all, coal. Bart dug up a piece of coal and started to grind it down with his chisel-like front teeth.

"That ought to do the trick," Bart said, and placed it into Satch the Copperhead Snake's mouth. Satch slithered down into the hole and gave Ranger Mike the pencil made of coal.

Ranger Mike knew the forest like he knew the back of his hand. He didn't need to see out of the hole to know where he was.

There was one problem. They had nothing to write the note on. "Wait. I know," Ranger Mike said, and ripped the pocket off his grey ranger shirt. He placed the piece of fabric on his thigh and scribbled down these words:

Mike folded the fabric and placed it in Satch's mouth, and Satch hurriedly squirmed out of the hole. "Just rest your head and we'll be back with help in no time,“ Ricky said.

Ranger Mike did just that. "Thank you," he said, "I think."

He was still quite confused by the whole scene, but he was even woozier from the fall. He took a deep breath and closed his eyes.

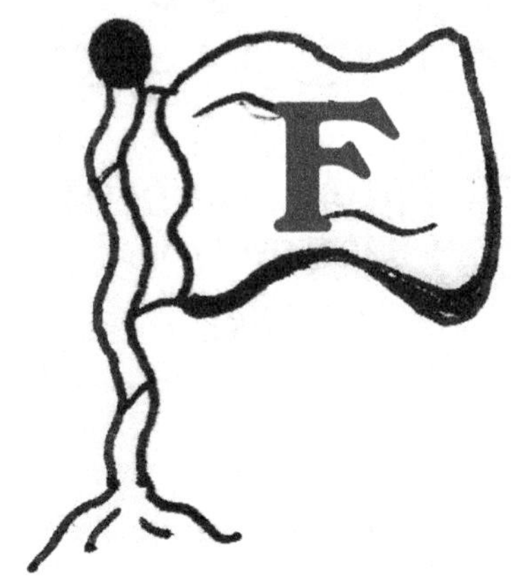

CHAPTER 3
Operation Friendship

Ricky stepped away from the hole and stopped suddenly. “One other thing,” he said, turning back to Ranger Mike, but he was asleep. “What is the matter, Ricky?” Satch asked.

“I don’t know the way to the Ranger Station. Does anybody?”

The animals responded with shrugged shoulders and blank stares.

“We can always wait until Ranger Mike wakes up,” Bart said.

“There isn’t time,” Ricky replied.

“Wait a minute,” Satch said. “We’ll give the note to a flock of birds. They will be able to spot the Ranger Station from the sky. We’ll get help to Ranger Mike in no time,“ he said confidently.

The animals looked up. The trees were very quiet. There wasn’t a bird in sight. “That is strange. Where are they? I don’t see a bluebird, a sparrow, not even, dare I say, a hawk.”

All the animals cringed at the very sound of the word. Many of the forest creatures were not the best of friends with hawks because, like Tombstone, they found themselves on the hawks’ dinner menu.

“Come to think of it, I don’t remember seeing a bird either,” Bart said. “In fact, I haven’t had to clean a single bird poop off my dam all day.”

“The Wind Dragon, that’s it,“ Shelby realized. “I bet they have all flown to higher ground until it passes. It could be days before they return. We can’t wait that long!”

“You’re right,“ Ricky said with disappointment. “Now what do we do?”

“Hey, owls are great flyers. Maybe Wetherbee the Owl will help,” Barry said. Wetherbee grunted and slammed his front door shut.

“Or not.”

“Old Mr. Grumpy is at it again, I see,” Merlin the Owl said.

“Can you help, Merlin?” Ricky asked.

“I sure wish I could, Ricky,” he replied with a jolly laugh, “but these old wings don’t have much flight left in them. And even if they did, I doubt they could keep this jelly belly of mine in the air for very long.”

“Who are we kidding?” Bart said. “The birds were our only hope. We are just a bunch of stupid animals. We’re not smart enough to figure this out. Look at me. How am I going to come up with a plan to save Ranger Mike with a brain the size of a pea?”

“Yeah,” Satch agreed. “Mine is even smaller than that.”

All the animals shook their heads and agreed with Bart and Satch.

Merlin flew up to his perch and looked down. “So that’s it? You’re all going to quit? All because you don’t think you’re smart enough? Look at the humans. They have huge brains compared to ours, and they are always doing knuckleheaded things.

Like forgetting to put out their campfires or not knowing what poison ivy looks like and using it as toilet paper."

The animals grimaced and sat down.

"Well, that's true," Ricky said. "They don't seem to be all that bright."

"Yeah," said Shelby. "You have a point there."

"It is true, you may not be able to depend on the birds," Merlin said as he took off his glasses and cleaned them with a leaf, "but you can always depend on the 'magic' words."

"The magic words? What do you mean?" Ricky asked.

"The answer is within you, Ricky. It lies within all of you," Merlin said and replaced his glasses. "A beautiful rose cannot bloom by seed alone. Now, I think it is time for me to go and rest these old bones of mine."

The animals stared at each other with puzzled looks. "What could Merlin possibly mean?" They wondered.

"Magic words? I think the old owl is starting to lose it. The only magic words I can think of are 'pretty please with sugar on top and shredded coconut.' I can't imagine how that is going to help," Bart said.

"Wait," Shelby said as her ears perked up. "That's it!"

"What's it?" Ricky asked.

"Imagine. My grandfather always told me if I want my dreams to come true, all I need to do is follow my imagination. Those must be the magic words. A rose cannot bloom by seed alone. It needs fresh soil, water, and sunshine. By ourselves we may not be able to, but if we all put our imaginations together, I know we can come up with a way to save Ranger Mike."

"Shelby is right," Ricky said. "Think about it, guys. We can't fly through the forest, so we need to figure out another way."

"The stream," Satch said. "We can use the stream."

"Yes," Ricky replied.

"I got it!" Said Mongo the Muskrat. "Once I saw a group of humans place a note in a soda bottle and float it downstream."

"That is a good idea, Mongo, except for one thing: We don't drink soda. Where are we going to find a soda bottle?" Ricky said.

"I have a rad idea," said Bodhi the Frog. "I can't hang on air, but I can certainly boogie down the bone yard, baby." Bodhi was the coolest dude in the forest. Give him a surfboard made out of tree bark and he would, in his words, "head out on a sweet ride."

"Bone yard?" Bart wondered.

Bodhi might have been the coolest dude in the forest, but nobody ever knew what in the world he was talking about. He had a language all his own. The only one who could understand Bodhi was his brother Heywood. Everyone turned toward him for an answer.

"The bone yard is the rocks in the stream," Heywood explained. "He can't fly down the stream, but he can certainly hop."

"Righteous, dude," Bodhi said with a smile.

"Perfect, Bodhi," Shelby said, "and you can explain to the animals you see along the way that Ranger Mike is in need of their help."

"Yeah," said Bart, "and we can use their skills and talents to find the Ranger Station."

"This sounds like an awesome plan. We'll call it Operation Friendship," Ricky said. "If everyone pitches in, I know we can save Ranger Mike."

Before Ricky could give the note to Bodhi, an all too familiar and frightening voice interrupted their plan.

"Well, well, my furry little friends." The animals' bones rattled with fear. Nobody wanted to turn around. They knew that once they did, they would find themselves staring into the eyes of their worst nightmare, Tombstone.

"Why wasn't I invited to the party? I'm starting to feel as if you guys don't like me," he said with a sinister laugh. He then noticed the hole in the ground around which the animals had gathered. "What do we have here?"

The animals did not put up a fight. They quickly cleared a path for Tombstone, and he walked toward the edge of the hole.

Ricky knew Ranger Mike was not in danger. Mountain lions are powerful leapers, but it was obvious to Ricky, by the bulge in Tombstone's belly, that he had just eaten. There was no way he would be able to get in and out of the hole until the food had digested. Even a mountain lion couldn't win a battle when trapped.

What did concern Ricky was the note. If Tombstone caught him with the note, not only would he tear it apart, but there was a good chance he would tear him apart as well.

He dropped the note to the ground, covered it with dirt, and nudged it over to Mongo the Muskrat with his back paw. He glanced at Mongo and nodded ever so gently. Mongo nodded back. He knew exactly what Ricky wanted him to do. He needed Mongo to hide the note . . . and muskrats could float under water for quite a long time.

Mongo placed the note in his mouth to keep it dry and backed ever so gently down the bank of the stream. He accidentally kicked up a pebble while doing so. It rolled down and – "doink"– landed in the water just as his head submerged.

Tombstone swung his head around. A mountain lion's ears are so sensitive, they can hear a leaf snap off a tree a mile away. "What was that?" He snarled, staring into Ricky's eyes.

"I'm sorry," Ricky said. "It was nothing. I just slipped and kicked a rock into the water."

Tombstone's lip began to quiver. "You're lying!" He said and took a step toward Ricky. The animals turned away and closed their eyes. They could not bear to watch.

Fortunately for Ricky, Ranger Mike made a jostling noise inside the hole. "I'll take care of you later," he said to Ricky and stepped over to the edge.

Tombstone's eyes lit up like a squirrel's in an acorn store. He slapped his tongue across his lips and said the words all the animals feared: "I offer you an invitation to dinner, Mr. Ranger: my dinner."

Unlike Ricky, Shelby didn't realize Ranger Mike was in no danger. She couldn't just stand by and let Tombstone do as he pleased. Ricky put up his paw to stop her, but it was too late. She stepped between Ranger Mike and Tombstone. The animals could not believe what Shelby was doing. None of the animals had the courage to stand up to Tombstone. They just cowered before him and did what he said. Hopefully, if they were lucky, really lucky, they would come away with their heads still attached.

"This is bad, really bad," they thought.

Shelby knew the risk, but she thought there had to be at least one good-hearted bone in Tombstone's body. She was about to find out there wasn't.

"Please, Mr. Lion," she begged. "It is Ranger Mike. Don't hurt him. He has done so much for us. We need to get him help."

A fearsome roar rocked the forest floor. "Silence!" Tombstone shouted. "Never tell me what I can or cannot do. Remember this, all of you! I'm the ruler of this forest. You do what I say, and I do what I please!"

Tombstone flicked a chunk of meat from between his teeth with his pinky claw. He lowered his head and flashed his bloodstained fangs right in front of Shelby's eyes. "Do I scare you?" He asked.

"A little," Shelby replied. But, to be honest, she didn't know what was worse: the fear of death or his wicked bad breath.

"Well, today is your lucky day, sweetheart. I already had lunch. My belly is quite full." He lifted his head and turned around. "You're all lucky. For now, that is."

Tombstone started walking back up the dirt path toward his lair. "You have until sundown to save your precious ranger," he said. "I will be back for my dinner." A thunder boomer echoed in the distance, followed by the first raindrops.

Tombstone stopped and glanced back over his shoulder. "That is, of course," he said with a sinister grin, "if the Wind Dragon doesn't get him first."

The animals didn't breathe a single breath until Tombstone faded from view. "That was close," Bart said. Everyone was quite relieved. "It's safe, Mongo," Ricky said.

Mongo splashed out of the water and crawled to shore, gasping for air. "Man, talk about cutting it close. I only had another 30 seconds," he said, breathing heavily. Bart patted him on the back for a job well done.

"Are you sure you are okay with this, Bodhi?" Ricky asked. "It could be quite dangerous."

"I'm ready to shred," he replied.

Everyone's eyes shifted to Heywood. "That would be a . . . yes," he said.

Mongo opened his mouth, and the note rolled onto his paw. Bodhi lashed out his tongue and snatched it up. He then turned around. "Later, dudes!" He shouted, tucked his surfboard under his arm and off he hopped.

Shelby turned around to face everyone. She felt awful for putting them in danger. "I'm sorry, everybody," Shelby apologized. "I thought for sure Tombstone would understand. I just made things worse."

Merlin the Owl flew down and propped himself up on a tree stump. "Oh heck, don't worry about that loud-mouth lion," he said. "Tombstone is nothing more than a great big bully. He might be bigger than us, but we're stronger than he is where it counts." Merlin tapped his heart. "Right here."

Merlin then turned and looked at Shelby and smiled, as if to say everything is okay. "Friends together, friends forever!" The animals cheered and threw their paws into the air.

Their team spirit was going to be put to the test, not only with Tombstone, but even more so with the Wind Dragon. The weather was getting spookier by the second. Thick, menacing clouds began to roll in over Mount Chubaluba, and the wind began to howl through the trees.

The animals realized they needed another plan, not only to protect Ranger Mike from the Wind Dragon, but to protect themselves, too.

After a short discussion, it was decided that Ricky, Shelby, Bart, Barry, and Satch would stay behind as long as possible with Ranger Mike. The others would head back to their families and try their best to defend themselves against the Wind Dragon's fury.

Bart and Barry quickly built a dam around the hole so groundwater would not pour in. Ricky, Satch, and Shelby then gathered up tree branches and placed them over the hole to protect Ranger Mike from any flying debris.

After securing the hole as well as possible, the five turned and looked down the stream. Bodhi was no longer in sight. "Do you think Operation Friendship stands a chance?" Bart asked.

"Yes, Bart," Ricky replied. "I know it does. We just have to believe."

CHAPTER 4
Boogie Down the Bone Yard

Bodhi's watery adventure started out easy enough, but after a while the water started to get rough, and he had to put the brakes on. The gentle stream flowed into the raging white waters of the Walla Wunga River. He realized he could no longer make it down the river by simply hopping from rock to rock. It would be much too dangerous. If he slipped, the river would swallow him whole.

"Surf's up!" He said and dropped his surfboard into the water. "Time to rock and roll freestyle!"

Bodhi took a deep breath, squatted down, and let the rapids be his guide. Most animals would have been scared out of their minds, but for Bodhi, this was like a day at the beach. He weaved his way around the bone yard with the swiftness and ease of a master video gamer.

Even a tree that had fallen across the river was no match for his groove. He left his surfboard and leaped over the broken-down tree. "Gnarly, baby," he said as he wiggled his toes and flapped his arms, or in surfer terms, hobble-bobbled in the air.

The board floated out from under the tree, and Bodhi landed back on without skipping a beat.

Though he had mastered the river to this point, he was still far from being out of the watery woods. A series of cascading waterfalls were up next. Bodhi didn't blink an eye: He styled each fall with ease until the last cascade. He slid off a flat rock hidden just below the water and tumbled out of control.

"Wow!" He shouted as he flipped through the air.

When it seemed he was certain to fall into the river, a blue and silver light flashed before his eyes, and he felt a gentle breeze blow across his rubbery skin. Instead of falling into the raging water, the breeze allowed him to catch his balance, and he landed butt first on his surfboard.

"High five to the Big Kahuna!" He shouted. The Big Kahuna was considered by surfers to be the god of sun, sand, and waves. The high five was his way of thanking the Big Kahuna or whatever had helped him a moment ago. "It's been a great ride, but I think it be time to bail," he realized, not wanting to press his luck.

He looked toward shore for some type of life, but there was no one around. "Hmm . . . something is not right," he thought as he stood back up on the board. He had a bad feeling in his belly. Not only were there no animals, but the river was picking up speed at an incredible pace.

Bodhi knew this could mean only one thing. The mother of all waterfalls was waiting for him on the other side of the bend: the Razor's Edge Falls. He had never seen it, but every animal in the forest knew about it. More important, they knew to stay clear of it.

To be safe, the rangers posted warning signs all along the river. Bodhi read each one as he passed by.

And most nerve-wracking of all . . .

The rapids and waterfall were dangerous enough, but what swam in the water below the waterfall is what gave the fall its rather ominous name. The water was home to a school of northern pike that grew six feet in length. Some fish tales suggested they were closer to ten feet.

The northern pike were the most feared predators of the Walla Wunga River. Their razor-sharp teeth could chew through a license plate as if it were a waffle. The waterfall was the pikes' personal room service buffet. They simply swam up and their dinner dropped down.

Bodhi was wise to the danger. He noticed a tree branch that dangled out across the river. "I'm outta here," he said, and reached up with his sticky fingers, thinking he could easily grasp hold. Little did he know that the tree branch was brittle and old, and when he reached out, it snapped off. "This is not good," he said, staring at the broken branch. It was his last chance. There was nothing but whitewater between the waterfall and him.

"Way cool," he said with surprise as he came around the bend. It wasn't what he expected. "This might not be a bummer after all." The mist from the fall had created a brilliant-colored rainbow. "How can something so gnarly be dangerous?" He thought.

Bodhi splashed through the rainbow, tucked his legs inward, and sailed over the fall. "Look out below!" He shouted. "Cannonball!"

He plunged into the water and sunk like a stone to the bottom. On his way up through the murky water, he saw a number of shadowy figures quickly approaching. When the water cleared a bit, he realized the fish tales were wrong. The pike weren't ten feet long; they were twenty feet long!

"Get him, boys! Frog legs for dinner!" Shouted Louie the Pike.

Bodhi swam like an eel toward the surface of the river. He splashed out of the water and frantically looked around. He could feel the pike family closing in on him. "There," he said. A rock was just a few feet away. He swam over and crawled onto the rock just as Louie leaped out of the water.

Bodhi tried pulling himself farther up, but his right leg slipped and splashed back down. Louie's mouth watered with delight as the delicious treat dangled before his eyes.

Louie snapped down hard with his razor-sharp teeth, expecting a mouthful of meat. Instead, all he got was air. "Sorry, dude, no food for you," Bodhi said and lifted his leg clear.

Though he had outwitted Louie, Bodhi knew there was no time to gloat. He was still in a real pickle. The winds were getting stronger, and it would only be a matter of time before his tiny body would blow over the edge of the rock. With Louie and his gang circling below, he had to come up with a plan. And fast.

"Should I make a swim for it?" He thought. The shore was only twenty feet away. If he timed it correctly, maybe, just maybe, he could out swim Louie and his gang.

Before he could make a decision, the rock began to shake. Louie dropped down and stuck to the rock with his sticky webbed feet. "Holy mcmoly!" He said.

"Sorry about that. Didn't know anyone was up there," responded a deep but calming voice. Bodhi stood up and looked all around. Nobody was there. "Down here, young fella."

Boy, was Bodhi ever relieved! He wasn't standing on a rock. It was a turtle shell.

"My name is Timothy T. Turtle. But my friends call me the Ripper, on account of the fact I rip up the water with my speed."

Now it is true, Timmy might not have been as fast as a gazelle, or even a slug for that matter, but to the other turtles in the Walla Wunga River, he was greased lightning.

"Nice to meet you, Timmy. My name is Bodhi. Would you mind shooting me to shore? I need to find help. Ranger Mike wiped out and is hurt badly."

Timmy didn't have to think twice. "Ranger Mike is hurt? Why, you bet I'll help! Mike and all the rangers have my utmost respect. They stopped hunters from fishing the river for my family, friends, and me. Why, if it wasn't for the rangers, I'd be nothing more than a bubbling bowl of turtle stew on a human's dinner table."

Just then Bodhi noticed Louie's fin rise out of the water. "But I don't want to put you in danger," Bodhi said.

Timmy chuckled. "Don't you worry, there is nothing to fear. His brother Rummy tried to take a bite out of me once."

"What happened?"

"Well, to make a long story short, they now call him Gummy."

They both laughed. “Now fasten your seat belt and hang on, my friend,” Timmy said. “I have a need for speed!”

Timothy put on his racing goggles, lunged back, and chug-a-lugged his way toward shore, to the dismay of Louie the Pike.

Twenty minutes later, Bodhi leaped off Timmy’s shell and splashed his way to land. “Good luck finding help!” Timmy said.

“I’ll do my best,” Bodhi replied. “Thanks for the ride.”

Luck was something Bodhi would need lots of. “Bummer, it’s a dead end,” he said. Nothing but trees were in front of him. He couldn’t risk hopping into the forest on his own and getting lost.

“The only thing I can do is continue down the edge of the river,” he thought, hoping to find someone who could help along the way. After hopping for what seemed like an hour, he finally heard signs of life. He leaped onto a large boulder and looked out. A colony of female rabbits were drinking from a shallow pool of water.

“What’s up, dudettes?” He said.

“May I help you?” A rabbit named Marge asked, a little confused by his choice of words.

“A ranger wiped out hanging five over the sky.”

The rabbits turned and looked at each other. “Um, excuse me?” Marge said.

Bodhi realized they didn’t understand a word he was saying. Without his brother alongside to interpret, he knew he had to, in his words, “channel down the vocab.”

“Oh, sorry,” he said. “A ranger is badly hurt and in need of help.”

“Oh my! What happened?”

“He fell from the sky and isn’t able to walk. I have been sent on a mission to ask the animals of the forest for their help in finding the Ranger Station. The mission is called Operation Friendship."

Bodhi spat out his tongue, gave Marge the note, and she read it aloud.

Out of the pack stepped a rabbit named Dani. "Last spring, after a windstorm, Ranger Mike helped my dad and me break free from under a fallen tree. I don't know where the Ranger Station is, but I will do whatever I can to help. It's the least I can do for Ranger Mike and his family."

Marge gave the note to Dani. "Thank you for your help!" Bodhi said. She smiled.

Bodhi watched as Dani disappeared into the sea of trees. "Well, time to catch a wave back home," Bodhi said.

"Safe travels," Marge replied.

CHAPTER 5
King of the Mountain

Dani stuck the note in the fold of her fur as she weaved in and out of the trees and bushes. She hopped up the largest hill she could find and looked out across an open field. The Ranger Station was nowhere in sight.

"There has to be a faster way!" Just then, she looked overhead and saw a pack of squirrels swinging through the pine trees. Dani whistled to catch their attention.

A squirrel named James quickly rushed down the trunk of the tree and raced to her side. Dani explained the dilemma at hand. "My mom says that we should all pitch in when others need help," he replied after hearing the bad news.

"Yeah," agreed his older sister Skylar from a branch above. "We'll spread the word. So don't worry. If the Ranger Station's out there, we'll easily spot it from the sky."

Skylar and James told their family and friends, who in turn told their family and friends about Operation Friendship. Suddenly, hundreds of squirrels were looking high and low for the Ranger Station.

Skylar and James crawled up to the top of the tallest pine tree they could find. The tree was so tall it was just a squirrel's tail away from the puffy grey storm clouds that were moving swiftly across the sky.

They stepped out to the edge of a limb and looked out. They thought for sure they would see the Ranger Station, but it was nowhere to be found. All that stood before them was a humongous mountain named Mount Lulu.

"It must be on the other side of the mountain," James said.

Just like Bodhi, they had reached a dead end. The mountain was just too rugged for them to climb. "It would take us forever and a day," James said.

Skylar bowed her head. "We'd better go back and tell Dani the bad news."

"Wait a minute," James said, "Maybe there's hope after all!"

James took out a pair of broken binoculars he found in the woods. Once, a birdwatcher accidentally dropped them on a rock and left them behind. He squinted through the one good lens. "I know who can help!" He said.

Skylar rolled her eyes. James loved his superheroes, especially the crime-fighting duo of Wonder Wasp and Super Skunk. "Forget it, James. A superhero is not going to come to our rescue," she said.

"No, no. This is for real!" He said, pointing to the base of the mountain. "Take a look for yourself."

She reluctantly took the binoculars and squinted through the lens. To her surprise, James was right! Hope wasn't lost.

Out of the tall weeds appeared Earl the Mountain Goat. Mountain goats were great climbers. Their soft, padded hooves were rimmed with sharp edges, making it easy for them to climb ice, rock, and even snow.

Earl was considered the best climber of his day. In fact, he had been crowned King of the Mountain ten years straight. This was a mountain goat record that, to this day, has never been broken.

Skylar was as confident as could be. "You're right, James! Earl can help. I know he can!"

They scurried down the pine tree and across the field as fast as they could. "Earl!" They yelled at the top of their lungs.

Earl was lunching on some straw near a brook when he heard his name. "Whoa there, my friends," he said. "What is the trouble?"

Skylar and James couldn't get a word out. They were pooped.

"Relax and drink some water," he laughed. "That will bring your voice around." They both slopped down a few sips of water and then explained to Earl about Operation Friendship.

"Ranger Mike is a good man," Earl said. "We go way back. Why, I remember him when he was your age. He is the spitting image of his dad. The well-being of the forest has always come first to Mike and his family. Those pine trees you guys love to play in? Well, years ago, a team of lumberjacks wanted to cut them down and build a fancy resort. It was what they called 'prime real estate.' Ranger Mike and his dad stopped them from doing so. We are very lucky to have a man like that looking out for us."

Earl limped forward and looked up the mountainside, his bones crackling with each step.

Skylar became a little concerned. She looked over at James. They were both thinking the same thing. At his age, he would never make it up the mountain. Like Merlin's wings, his legs had seen better days.

"The old goat will never make it," James whispered to Skylar.

"I heard that," Earl said.

James felt really bad. "I'm sorry, I didn't mean it," he said.

"Yeah, he didn't," Skylar agreed as she whacked her brother in the head with her tail. "He's always saying stupid things."

"Oh, it's okay. The young lad is right. I'm not as young as I used to be. And to be honest, I don't know if I have another climb in these old bones of mine. But there is an old saying my grandpa taught me years ago. He said, 'Earl . . .

...The journey might be long
The pain in my bones quite strong
But I would rather lie here and die
Than breathe another breath
knowing I did not try.' "

Skylar retrieved an acorn that was hidden in her cheek. She wrapped the note around the nut and tossed it to the ground. Earl bent down and picked up the nut with his two remaining teeth.

"Before I go, I must tell you," Earl said. "I do not remember a Ranger Station on the other side of Mount Lulu. At least not one I could see. The forest is quite thick with evergreens. There is barely enough room for a snake to slither through. However, I have an old friend who lives there. His name is Grey Wolf. There is no doubt in my mind he will be able to track down the Ranger Station."

Earl took a deep breath and lugged his tired old body up the mountain. "I'll see you on the other side," he said jokingly. Skylar and James wished him good luck and waved good-bye.

About halfway to the top, his old bones began to cause him discomfort. He had no other choice but to stop. He squatted down and rested for a moment. He looked up to see how far he still had to go. He could not believe his weary eyes.

"Okay, who's the wise guy that keeps raising the mountain?" He chuckled with a tired breath.

It would have been very easy for him to say, "That's it, I've had enough." But not Earl. He took his grandpa's words to heart. He was a champion climber for a reason. There may have been a lot of pain in his old bones, but there was no quit.

He lifted his hide and continued up the mountainside. Luckily for him, the rain that was now pouring down on the other side of the forest had not reached Mount Lulu. The mud would have made it almost impossible for his worn hooves to dig in. What wasn't so lucky was the fierce wind, but it just made him more determined to climb.

"This mountain is mine!" He said with pep in his stride. "There is no way you're going to blow me down!"

After a long hard struggle, Earl finally made it to the mountain peak. He turned back and looked across the valley toward the pine trees. Skylar, James, and their family and friends were bowing to him from the branches, shouting, "THE KING IS BACK! THE KING IS BACK!" Earl couldn't help but smile.

He waved and then climbed over the peak and looked out across the valley below. It was exactly how he remembered it to be, tree after tree after tree.

Earl eased his way down the side of the mountain to a clearing. "Let's see if these old bones still have the groove," he said and started to dance. A passing chipmunk had to do a double take as Earl wiggled his butt.

"Oh, momma! That's a sight no warm-blooded animal needs to see," the chipmunk said.

Earl was doing the mountain goat's version of hip-hop. "Got my wiggle. Gotta find my jiggle," he sang as his hooves flipped up and down and his tail spun around.

Wolves are very strong and powerful animals, but they are also quite light on their paws. When it came to dancing, wolves were considered the original party animals. They were known to get down with the "howling boogie" all night long. But there was also a very serious tone to their dancing. They used dancing as a way to warn each other. They could tell by the vibrations on the ground whether an animal in the distance was a friend or foe.

"I have not felt that rhythm in ages," a voice spoke. "Yet, it still brings a smile to my face." Earl looked up. A pack of wolves appeared out of the high grass.

"Running Wolf?" Earl asked. "Is that you?" Running Wolf was Grey Wolf's son.

"Yes, my friend. It's me. It has been a long time," Running Wolf said.

"Yes, it has. Much too long," Earl replied. "Look at you, all grown up and leader of your own pack. Like father, like son."

"Yes. I owe it all to Father. He taught me well."

"And speaking of your father, how is the old fella?" "Father is retired. His days of roaming have given way to afternoon naps." They both laughed. "And he much prefers spending time with his grand-wolves. 'They keep breath in my lungs and youth in my heart,' he says."

"I'm sure indeed," Earl said. "Your father is very wise. I learned a lot from him during my many years of climbing. Tell him I say hello. I'm sorry to have missed him."

"I will pass along your thoughts. Now, what brings you to our corner of the forest? I sense you do not travel with good news."

"It isn't, Running Wolf. It's Ranger Mike. He's been injured in a fall. We need to get him help before the Wind Dragon gets the better of him. I'm in search of the Ranger Station. I knew if anyone could lead us down the right path, it would be you and your family."

“My father and I have endless respect for Ranger Mike. He is a man of great honor. Like you, I feel in my heart that he is as much family as my own son,” he said.

“The Wind Dragon, on the other hand, has no honor. It is an angry spirit with senseless pride. I shall go and find this place called the Ranger Station. The rest of my pack shall stay here and help you back down the mountain.“

“How will you know which road to travel?“ Earl asked.

“Like my father before me, I will follow the spirit of the forest, and it shall be my guide,“ Running Wolf replied.

CHAPTER 6
Nurse Shelby

The Wind Dragon's fury picked up in intensity. Bart the Beaver realized that covering the hole with branches simply would not do the trick. He sliced off a piece of the parachute with his sharp front teeth, and he and Barry laid it over the hole while Ricky and Shelby rolled rocks onto the edges of the parachute to keep it from blowing away.

"That should hold for now," said Ricky, wiping the pouring rain from his eyes.

Shelby tucked two sturdy branches under her front leg, slipped under the parachute, and climbed down into the hole. She also brought with her a wound-up roll of grapevines.

Ranger Mike woke to find her wrapping the vines around his injured right leg. She was using the branches as a splint.

"Try not to move your leg," Shelby said with a smile. "Nurse's orders."

Ranger Mike smiled back. "Yes, ma'am," he replied.

Ranger Mike was very impressed by her nursing skills. Shelby was setting the splint as if she had been doing it for years.

Ranger Mike, like all rangers, had had to learn first aid as part of his training, just in case he came across an injured hiker or someone hurt in a fall. "You do that quite well," he said.

"Thank you," she replied.

"You're in good hands," said Satch, as he popped his head into the hole.

"Shelby takes care of all of us when we get sick or hurt. From the sniffles to a broken paw, Shelby is the best. My daughter Lily Grace sliced her skin on a sharp rock. It made my heart break to see her in pain. Shelby wrapped her up in a big green leaf and had her rest. Two days later, Lily Grace was slithering around like nothing ever happened."

"Thank you, Satch," she said. "But to be completely honest,. I'm not really a nurse."

"Well, after the talking thing, I figure anything is possible," said Mike. "How did you learn to splint a leg like that?"

"My family and I are from the nearby town of Wellington."

"Sure. I know it very well."

"We lived in a red maple tree right next to the nursing school. I have ten brothers and sisters. Like all squirrel families, we spent our days chasing each other up trees and collecting nuts for winter. One day, while playing, I stopped to catch my breath on a window seal at the nursing school. A human, they called her Jeanine, was teaching a class. I believe she called it first aid."

"Yes," Mike replied. "All of our rangers have to take Jeanine's class. In the forest, it is not always easy to get help quickly, so a ranger needs to know how to take care of someone by using nothing more than what Mother Nature gave us."

"Yeah. It was really cool. Every day for a month I would stop and listen to her speak. I learned a lot from Jeanine."

At that moment, Shelby lowered her head, and a tear trickled from her eye. "What is the matter?" Ranger Mike asked.

"Well, just before the end of the summer, something awful happened. The people who ran the nursing school were getting complaints about there being too many of us squirrels running around. The school hired a hunter named Harley. Harley trapped us in cages to, in his words, 'get rid of the vermin.' "

Mike grimaced as he lifted himself to a more comfortable position. "I know Harley quite well. He is rotten to the bone, and just as selfish. He thinks he can hunt and fish whenever and wherever he wants. He even uses the forest as a place to dump his trash. Most of us humans are very dedicated when it comes to following rules, especially the rules of nature, but there are a few, like Harley, who give the rest of us a bad name."

Shelby took a deep breath and continued her story. "First, Harley clipped off some of our tails to keep as souvenirs. I was one of the lucky ones," she said, lifting her fully grown and fluffy tail for him to see. "I learned about a plant in the forest used to help stop bleeding and make pain go away, but it didn't make Harley go away. He then put us into cages and drove us deep into the Walla Wunga Forest. It was a very bumpy ride, and one of the cages fell off the back of the truck. My little brother David was in the cage. We all felt so hopeless as we drove away. There was nothing any of us could do." Shelby bowed her head. "It was the last time we ever saw him. I would give anything just to know he is okay. My family and I miss him so much."

"Well, with you as his big sister, I'm betting he is fine," Ranger Mike said. "As for Harley? If there's one thing I have learned over the years, it's that Mother Nature has a way of getting even. I have a feeling she'll be knocking on Harley's door very soon."

Shelby smiled. "I hope so. Funny thing is, I thought I would always miss my old neighborhood, except for the cars, that is." They both chuckled. "But this is home now. I have a great family and wonderful friends. I couldn't ask for anything more."

Suddenly, the ground began to shake. Dirt, branches, and leaves fell into the hole. Outside, two powerful lightning bolts zapped across the sky. They crossed paths and exploded on impact, leaving behind a giant…

In the eyes of the animals of Walla Wunga Forest, it could only mean one thing: The X was a warning of doom. They were about to feel the wrath of the Wind Dragon's revenge. A blast of thunder followed, only it sounded more like a sinister laugh.

Many of the animals freaked out. They dropped what they were doing, abandoned their homes, and made a mad dash for the safety of the thicker forest. Or so they hoped. "Run for your lives!" They shouted. "The Wind Dragon is coming!"

Ricky poked his head into the hole. "What's all the racket out there?" Shelby asked.

Ricky paused. "Just lightning," he replied. He didn't want Ranger Mike to know the truth. He figured learning that animals could talk was enough for one day. If he told Ranger Mike a Wind Dragon was twisting through the forest seeking revenge, the ranger would probably think Ricky and all the animals were what they ate: nuts.

"Your mom is calling, Shelby. You need to go home," Ricky said. Shelby quickly knotted the vine to keep the splint in place. Ranger Mike thanked Shelby for her help, and she climbed out of the hole. "We will be back with help in no time, Ranger Mike," Ricky said, with Bart and Barry at his side.

"Don't worry about me. I'll be fine. Now go. All of you tend to your families."

Although things seemed bleak, a bit of good news was about to be uncovered. Ollie the Weasel and his brother Wart were out gathering weeds for their family burrow when Ollie noticed a glowing red light coming from the ground.

"Do you see that, Wart?" Ollie shouted. The wind was blowing so fiercely, they could barely hear each other.

"Yeah. What do you think it is?" Wart asked.

"Only one way to find out," Ollie replied, and he started to dig through the soggy grass.

"Help me," he said to his brother. A large piece of tree bark was in the way. Ollie and Wart each grabbed an edge and flipped the bark over, revealing the best news they could have ever imagined. "What is it?" Ollie asked.

Wart took a closer look. "I think it is Ranger Mike's cell phone," Wart said. "I've seen campers using them."

"We have to get this to Ricky – and fast," Ollie said. "Ranger Mike can call for help in no time."

"Oh, baby! This is going to give us some serious forest cred, Ollie. They'll probably throw a parade for us," Wart said.

"Let's not worry about that. Just give me a hand."

They reached for the phone and it turned on. Ollie jumped back. A goofy face with giant, rotting teeth popped onto the screen. "Awesome," Wart said. "Doctor Grunge!"

“ Doctor who?” Ollie replied without a clue.

“Seriously, Ollie? It’s called a phone app. I’ve seen campers playing the game around the campfire. It’s really cool. You get to fix zombies’ teeth and win prizes.”

“Sounds kind of gross to me. No, thanks!”

“It’s fun. Here, let me show you.” Wart reached out to touch the screen.

“No!” Ollie shouted and pulled his brother away. “Just leave it be. I don’t want to break it. Let’s go back and tell the others.”

Before they could take a step, a cold, dark shadow crept over them. Neither had to turn around to know what was behind them.

“Well, well, what do we have here?” Tombstone asked in a bitter tone of voice.

Ollie and Wart slowly turned. Before Ollie could get a word out, Wart started singing like a canary. “It is Ranger Mike’s phone, Mr. Tombstone. Humans use it to talk to one another far, far away. We were going to go and find you and give it to you, honest we were.”

Ollie looked at his brother in disbelief. “Wart!” He grunted through his teeth.

“Sorry, Ollie. What can I say? It’s in my blood. I’m a weasel.”

Tombstone stepped over to the phone. “So Ranger Mike can call for help, you say? Isn’t that just wonderful? Of course, I would be out of a delicious dinner.” He then turned his head toward Ollie and Wart. “That is, unless the two of you would like to take his place.” They didn’t say a word. “I didn’t think so. Besides, you two are more like a midday snack than dinner.”

Tombstone scooped up the phone with his paw.

“This shall remain our little secret,” Tombstone said. All Ollie and Wart could do was shake their heads yes. “I thought you would agree.”

To do anything else would have meant certain doom for the both of them and their family. Tombstone placed the phone between his teeth and walked away. Any hope Ranger Mike had of making it to safety now lay solely with Running Wolf.

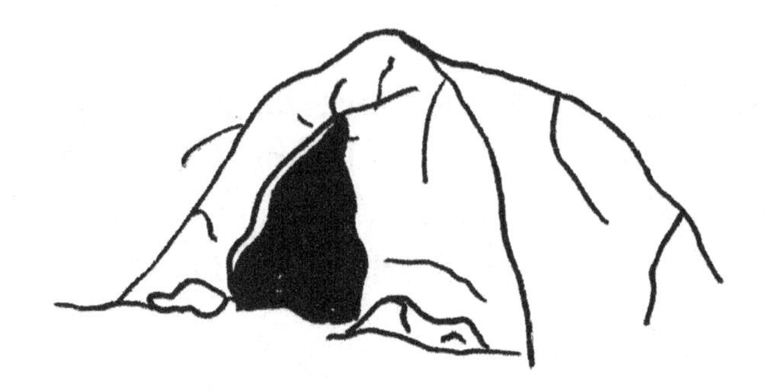

CHAPTER 7
The Phantom of the Forest

Earl knew, as he watched Running Wolf begin his journey, it would not be easy for him. Wolves relied heavily on scent to make their way safely through the forest. With the winds blowing stronger and rain starting to fall, his sense of smell would be hampered, making the dense forest much more dangerous, even for an experienced tracker like Running Wolf.

Not only was the lack of scent a problem, but the path he traveled was lined with all kinds of unpredictable dangers. One second he could be walking on flat ground, and the next second his paws could drop out from underneath and he could find himself tumbling down a cliff. If he was lucky, there would only be a few cuts and bruises. If he was unlucky, well, let's just say many animals had entered into this area of the forest and were never seen or heard from again.

"If anyone can make it through to the other side, it will be my son."

Earl turned to find Grey Wolf approaching.

"It is wonderful to see you again, Grey Wolf," Earl said, greeting him with a smile.

"Likewise. It has been too long, my friend. I only wish it were under happier circumstances," said Grey Wolf.

"Yes, indeed," said Earl as he turned and looked toward Running Wolf. "I have great faith in your son. You have taught him well, Grey Wolf. He is truly a leader of great honor and courage."

"He is the best I've seen in my many years, and I don't say that just because he is my son," Grey Wolf said. They both laughed. "Honor and courage are powerful traits, but only combined with a humble heart can one do great things. It is, and shall forever be, the code of the wolf."

Earl and Grey Wolf stood side by side and watched as Running Wolf disappeared into the trees.

For Running Wolf, there would be no dancing this day. This was serious business. He had to focus on each and every step he took. Running Wolf had told Earl he would "let the spirit of the forest" be his guide. That spirit was his instincts. With his sense of smell limited, those instincts would be more important than ever. To allow his mind to wander, even for one brief moment, could cost him dearly.

He squeezed through a pair of evergreens and suddenly stopped. The trees in front of him were leaning forward. His instincts told him to back away. "The tree roots have nothing to hold onto," he thought.

He followed his instinct and circled around the trees. The spirit of the forest guided him well. There was no ground on the other side. The roots of the trees were dangling over a cliff that dropped down as far as his eyes could see.

"That was close," Running Wolf thought.

A short distance later the trees opened up. "Mother Nature's amazing artistry," Running Wolf said.

Moments before he had encountered the dark side of the forest, and now he was consumed by all its beauty. Standing before him was a colorful field of yellow, peach, red and orange lilies. Beyond the field of lilies stood a magnificent mountain of stone. "Truly awe-inspiring," he thought as he made his way through the lily field. As he approached the mountain of stone, he became a bit concerned. The mountain had many tunnels.

"One of these caves must lead to the Ranger Station," he thought, "but which one?"

As he pondered which path to follow, he noticed a big, black, burly bear named Buford sitting on a log outside one of the caves. "Bears hibernate in caves all winter long. If anyone would know which way to go, it would be him," Running Wolf thought.

He galloped over to the side of Buford. "Hello there," he said with a howl. His voice caught Buford by surprise.

"Ahhhhhh!" Buford screamed, his face full of fear, and leaped a mile into the air.

"Sorry to have scared you, my friend," apologized Running Wolf.

"Scared? You thought I got scared?" Said Buford, "Oh no, no, no!"

He was spooked, but the last thing he wanted was for Running Wolf to know the truth. Black bears were revered for their strength and courage.

"I was just . . . exercising is all," Buford said as he leaped into a set of jumping jacks. "There is a long winter ahead and a bear has to keep in shape, you know."

"Oh, okay," Running Wolf said. "Well then, my friend, since you are in such good shape, I am in need of your help. I must get this message through to the Ranger Station." He lifted the note for Buford to see. "I believe it is on the other side of this mountain of stone. Do you know these caves very well?"

"Know them? Why, I could do cartwheels through them," he said boastfully.

"Good. Then I need you to travel through to the other side and get help."

"Hummina, hummina," Buford mumbled with terror in his eyes. "But, but, it is awfully dark in there."

"You aren't afraid of the dark, are you?" Running Wolf asked.

"Who? Me? Afraid? Are you kidding? Why, I'm the most fearless animal in the forest," Buford said proudly. He was actually telling the truth. He wasn't afraid. He was petrified.

It wasn't so much the darkness that frightened Buford; it was what lived in the darkness. According to folklore, an evil, red-eyed night creeper known as the Phantom of the Forest haunted the caves. The story was quite similar to the legend of the evil, red-eyed monster that children believed hid in the shadows under their beds.

Like children, most bears lost their fear of ghosts and monsters as they grew up. Buford was not like most bears: He believed as strongly in the Phantom today as he had when he irst heard the terrifying tale, while sitting around a campfire with his fellow cubs.

It had been almost midnight, and the moon was passing in and out of the clouds. Perfect for a ghost story, the bear elders thought. The tale of the Phantom had the cubs clinging together, their teeth clattering with fear. The scariest part of the story came at the very end. The elders stood up and warned the cubs, "There is but one way to survive. Get out of the dark and into the light before you are eaten alive." It was at that point that the rest of the bear elders had jumped out of the darkness, scaring the wits out of Buford and his fellow cubs.

Though it was just harmless hijinks, Buford never forgot those words. He wouldn't go any farther than the entrance to the cave, making sure to stay within striking distance of the moonlight.

While the other bears of the forest kicked back in their caves and snoozed all winter long, Buford curled up in the corner of the entrance way with his eyes wide open, fearing the Phantom would snatch him if he dozed off. He would even go so far as to use twigs to hold open his eyelids.

Running Wolf gave Buford the note and wished him safe travel.

"You mean you're not coming with me?" Buford asked.

"Sorry, my work here is done. I need to get back to my wolf-pack," he said.

"Oh dear," Buford mumbled. "I'm in real trouble." He was triple-terrified, but he couldn't back down and embarrass himself in front of Running Wolf.

Every bone in his body rattled with fear as he tiptoed into the dark cave. A few feet into his frightful trip, his body froze. A pair of glowing red eyes flashed open wide before the tip of his nose.

Buford didn't dare bother to say hello. "Ahhhhhhh!" He screamed at the top of his lungs. "The Phantom of the Forest! He's going to get me!"

Buford turned around and shot out of the cave as fast as a flaming arrow. He ran past Running Wolf, tripped over a rock, somersaulted into the path of a porcupine, rolled through a mud puddle, flipped back up, and buried his head in a tree trunk.

To add to his misery, the tree trunk happened to be home to Queen Bertha the Bumblebee. Needless to say, she was not very happy. "Look what you did to my hive," she said. With a face full of anger, she lifted up her stinger and stung him right between the eyes.

Buford was in an awful state. Not only was he terrified, but his fur was all muddy, his head was throbbing, and he had a thousand porcupine quills sticking out of his butt.

"What is the matter?" Running Wolf asked.

"It was horrible, I tell you, just horrible. These big red spooky eyeballs were staring at me. It was the Phantom of the Forest, I tell you," he said.

"The Phantom of the Forest?" Running Wolf asked. "There are no such things as phantoms. I'm sure all you saw were the eyes of a harmless bat. Why, you're not a fearless bear; you're nothing more than a little scaredy-cat."

"I'm not a scaredy-cat. I'm just very sensitive, that's all," Buford blubbered.

Running Wolf yanked the note from Buford. "Where are you going?" Buford asked.

"Where does it look like I'm going? To the cave. I have no time for this silly nonsense."

"Before you go, could you help pull out these porcupine quills?" Buford asked as he popped his head out of the hive and bent over.

"My father always taught me to lend a helping paw to a fellow animal in need. It is the honorable thing to do. But I draw the line at pulling thorns of any kind from another animal's behind. You're on your own, my friend."

Running Wolf shook his head and entered the cave. It was dark and musty, but there was no sign of the legendary creature called the Phantom of the Forest. In fact, it wasn't even on Running Wolf's mind. He was more concerned with not getting lost. "A maze of stone," he thought. "I really could use some light."

His wish was granted in the form of a red light. Actually, there were two red lights to be exact. They were round with eyeballs in the center. The legend of the Phantom of the Forest was true. Well, sort of. "Who dares enter into my cave?" echoed an evil voice.

"Who are you?" Running Wolf demanded, his voice bouncing off the walls of the cave. "And don't give me any of this Phantom nonsense. You might be able to pull one over on poor Buford, but I will not fall for such a ridiculous tale."

The red eyes floated closer. Out of the darkness appeared just what Running Wolf had expected: It wasn't a Phantom or a ghost; it was the shadow of a bat. However, Running Wolf might have been better off if it were a phantom, for this was no ordinary bat. The evil red eyes belonged to Venula, the venomous vampire bat.

"You dare enter into my cave? What an unlucky fool. I'll give you three seconds to run or I shall suck all the blood out of you," she said with a flash of her fangs. Running Wolf wasn't afraid, but he also wasn't stupid. He didn't dare stick around and challenge a vampire bat on her home turf. He took off and didn't stop galloping until he made his way back to the entrance of the cave. The only thing was, it was a different entrance. He looked around for Buford, but he was nowhere to be seen.

"Hello," sounded a voice overhead. Running Wolf looked up. Dangling from a stalactite was another bat. This one, however, seemed quite friendly to Running Wolf.

"Hi, my name is Benji," he said as he flew down to greet Running Wolf. "I'm sorry for the way Venula treated you. She's just a mean old bat. Is there anything I can do to make it up to you?"

"I need to find my way through to the other side of the mountain," he said. He then explained Operation Friendship to him. Benji didn't have to think twice. He was eager to help.

"Maybe I should go alone. It's much safer to fly. These caves are filled with many twists and turns, even a few bottomless pits. It is also a long journey. It would take forever to walk."

"So it shall be," Running Wolf replied, and he thanked Benji for his kindness.

Benji tucked the note under his wing and flew through the cave as fast as he could. About an hour into his flight, he entered a portion of the cave that could only be described as a crystal palace. The icicle-like stalactites and stalagmites lit up with beautiful red, blue, green, and purple fluorescent colors. It was truly a magnificent sight. Benji figured this would be a good place to rest his weary wings before continuing on with the final leg of his journey. He hung upside-down from a purple stalactite, folded his wings, and closed his eyes.

His restful sleep was short-lived. "What is this I see, a bat double crossing me?" Venula snarled with startling surprise. Benji whipped open his eyes and tried to explain that he meant no harm. "No, Your Highness, Running Wolf needed our help. A ranger is in danger," he said, and lifted up the note for her to see. "It is called Operation Friendship. We all need to pitch in and try to find the Ranger Station."

"Oh, Operation Friendship, I see. That changes everything. Of course we will help," she said.

Benji wasn't buying any of it. He knew she was just toying with him. "I'm always up for helping. In fact, my foolish little friend, guess who is going to need the help now?" She then waved her wing forward. "GET HIM, BOYS!" She yelled in a sinister voice.

A pack of Venula's vampire goons flew toward Benji with their fangs flashing.

"Burn, baby, burn!" He said and took to flight.

"I need a plan if I'm going to keep my promise to Running Wolf, and I need it fast," he thought as he flew with fury through the cave, dodging stalagmites and stalactites at every turn. He tried his best, but he couldn't shake Venula's goons. Their wings were much bigger and stronger. He would weave around the stalagmites and stalactites, and the vampire bats would simply plow right through them.

He realized his only remedy would be to outsmart his enemy. Luckily for him, Venula's goons weren't very bright.

"Zelda! That's it! Zelda can help me!" He cried.

He flew into a dark tunnel, hoping it would give him the few extra seconds he needed to complete his plan. And it worked. Venula's goons lost sight of him momentarily. It was all the time Benji needed. He flew low to the ground, took a quick right, and headed for a distant, glimmering light. The light signaled the doorway to the outside.

Venula's goons quickly recovered and closed the gap. Benji whipped his wings with all the energy he had left. "Now!" He shouted. Just as he was about to fly into the light, he swung up and latched onto a stalactite in the hope Venula's goons would fly right by and into his trap. He got his wish and they did just that. Unlike Benji, they had no idea what was ahead. They flew through the light and into an icky, sticky spider web.

"Well, hello there, boys,“ said Zelda the Black Widow Spider as she crawled from her hole. "Care for a cup of tea?" Zelda may have been a black widow spider, but she was as friendly as could be, always there to offer up her hospitality.

"Zelda!“ Benji shouted.

"Oh, hello there, Benji," Zelda replied with a comforting smile. "How are you today, honey?"

"Much better now," he said as he watched Venula's goons angrily try to peel their way out of the sticky mess without success. They were also a bit anxious. They knew black widow spiders were notorious for liquefying their prey with their gnashing fangs and then slurping them down like a milkshake.

To make matters even worse, they had to fight their way out of the web with their eyes closed. Bats and sunlight went together like peanut butter and liver.

Benji flipped on a pair of shades and flew down to Zelda. "Do you know where the Ranger Station is?"

"Ranger Station?" She thought for a second. "Not really, Benji. Why do you ask?" Benji explained to her about the note and Operation Friendship. "Oh dear," she said. "We must do something. Maybe the other animals know. I'll gather them up and see."

The forest outside the cave was known as the Land of the Orphaned Animals. It had been created so that all the animals that lost their parents or wandered astray would have a safe and friendly place to stay.

"Thank you, Zelda," Benji said. He then turned to Venula's goons. "Hey, fellas," he said as he lifted out a few pairs of sunglasses and scissors. "Need a little help?"

"Yes. Yes. Yes. We'll even pay you back. We promise. You can trust us," they replied together with grins.

Benji knew there wasn't an ounce of sincerity in their grins. "NOT!" He said and tossed the sunglasses and scissors over his wings. Venula's goons looked back at him and grunted and growled.

"It doesn't pay to be mean, does it?" Benji said. There was

no way he was going to help them out. Their way of paying him back would be with a blood-sucking fang attack.

"Catch you later, dudes," he said and floated away on his back, whistling a musical tune.

CHAPTER 8
The Orphaned Animals

Zelda crawled over to an old dried-out redwood tree that had long since passed away. She climbed out to the edge of a branch and dangled down by a web.

The entire Land of the Orphaned Animals was aware of the Wind Dragon's revenge. Everyone was running about in a frenzy, doing their best to help each other fortify their holes and burrows.

The animals that lived in the LOA, as they liked to call it, may not have looked like one another or come from the same background, but make no mistake about it, they were family.

Once you entered the LOA, you were greeted with open arms. No questions asked. "You will always be welcomed here" would be the first words spoken. The animals knew, since they no longer had families of their own, that if they were to survive, they would have to rely on one another. This kinship formed an unbreakable bond between them.

Sure, like any family they had their quarrels and misunderstandings, but at the end of the day, like all brothers and sisters, their love for one another shone through.

"Everybody, please, may I have your attention?" Zelda said.

Nobody heard a word. Zelda was only three inches big and therefore did not have the loudest of voices.

"Maybe this will do the trick," she said. Zelda lifted the tips of her two front spider legs between her tiny fangs, took a deep breath, and blew out a whistle that was so loud even the earthworms covered their ears, and they didn't even have ears.

Everyone froze in their tracks and looked back toward Zelda. She smiled. "Now that's better. As I was saying, everybody please stop what you are doing for a moment and gather around. I have some very important news. Unfortunately, it's not good news."

The animals lined up in front of Zelda and listened very carefully as she explained what was happening. The news about Ranger Mike touched the hearts of all the orphaned animals. He and his fellow rangers meant a lot to the animals of Walla Wunga Forest, but for the orphaned animals it was much more personal.

The rangers of Walla Wunga Forest had rescued most of them. They knew that if it were not for Ranger Mike and his team's courage and dedication, they would still be wandering the forest alone.

"Does anyone know where the Ranger Station might be?" Zelda asked.

Jasper the Coyote stepped forward. "I don't know where the Ranger Station is," he said, "but I do know there is a farmhouse on the other side of the cliff. I'm sure someone there would help."

"That is a terrific idea, Jasper," said Zelda, "except for one thing. How are we going to get to the other side?"

Zelda's concern was very real. Not only was the other side of the cliff too far away, but the side they were on dropped so far down that if you rolled a boulder over the edge, you would never hear it hit the ground.

The only way to reach the cliff on the other side would be to fly. They faced the same dilemma as Ricky and his friends. The orphaned animals, however, didn't need a pep talk from Merlin to see the light. They had faced so many obstacles in their own lives that giving up simply wasn't an option. It wasn't even a thought in anyone's mind.

"There has to be a way. There has to be," Jasper said. "The rangers have done so much for us." He turned toward Mario the Moose. "Mario? Didn't a ranger remove glass from your hoof when you stepped on that broken bottle left behind by a camper?"

Mario nodded. "Yes, he did," he said, looking down at the scar.

"A ranger helped you too, David," he said. Shelby's little brother stepped out from behind Mario. Like Mario, he nodded yes as well.

"My leg got trapped in the cage when it fell off Harley the Hunter's truck. A ranger came to my rescue. I lost my family that day," David continued, holding back the tears, "but I found you guys. And for that I will be forever grateful. I have the rangers to thank for that."

"Even me," Jasper continued. "If it were not for Ranger Mike, I'm afraid I wouldn't be here. I lost my family when I was just a young pup. I was too young to fend for myself. Ranger Mike found me near a dried-out brook. I could barely walk. He gave me food to eat and water to drink. He nursed me back to health."

"And there's something even more important to remember," Annie the Antelope said, stepping forward. "If we don't get help, Ranger Mike's children will grow up without a dad. We've all been there. We know what it is like to be alone. I don't want them to go through what we went through, do you?"

The animals shook their heads.

"Well then, we need an idea and fast," Zelda said as a rumble of thunder echoed in the distance. "I'm afraid the Wind Dragon is not going to wait for us."

Rollo the Monarch Butterfly offered up his wings. Everyone thanked Rollo, but they knew he would never make it. The storm winds had started to blow in. Rollo could barely steady his wings just floating before them. He would never make the flight across the cliff.

"Everyone, close your eyes and think really hard," said Zelda. "There's an idea out there somewhere."

Rollo's wings were growing tired, so he settled down on Izzy the Warthog's nose to ponder a plan. They were all mighty lucky he did. Izzy's nose began to itch, and then it began to twitch. "Ahhhhhh-choo!" He sneezed.

Rollo went whirling through the air and sliced through Zelda's dangling web. Zelda plopped to the ground. Rollo smacked face first into the old redwood, fell, and landed on Zelda's head.

Izzy started to apologize when all of a sudden his eyes lit up. The answer was staring right at him. He looked to the redwood tree and then to the cliff, back to the tree and over to the cliff again.

"That's it!" Izzy declared.

"That's what?" Zelda said, gently removing Rollo.

"We can knock down this old tree and use it as a bridge. It's plenty long enough to reach the other side from here."

"That is a wonderful idea," said Annie. Everyone looked at each other and agreed.

Mario the Moose threw out his chest. "Way to go, bro," he said to Izzy. "Chest bump! Chest bump!"

Izzy was so excited he forgot Mario's chest was as solid as a brick wall. He leaped off the ground and SMACK! Izzy bounced off Mario like a super ball and was planted five feet under the ground. "Oops!" Mario said, and he dropped his tail into the hole. "Sorry about that, little buddy."

"No problem, big fella," Izzy said as he grabbed his tail and crawled out with stars spinning around his head. "No problem at all."

Even though the tree was old and brittle, it was still going to take a good whack to knock it down. There was only one animal that could handle the job: Tank the Buffalo. His mother named him Tank for good reason. Tank's head was twice as solid as Mario's chest.

Without a moment of hesitation, he lumbered fifty feet past the tree and turned around. Smoke snorted from his nose. "Let's rock!" He cheered through his thick black beard and rumbled forward. He planted his head right into the center of the tree's trunk, but it didn't give an inch.

"Oh no," said Jasper. All the animals let out a sigh.

Tank didn't seem nearly as concerned. He slapped his paws together and cracked his knuckles. "A little faith, my friends," he said as he turned around. Tank lifted up his tail, wiggled it, and let out one of his famous SBDs, a silent but deadly wave of gas that was no match for the old redwood.

"Tank, I never thought I would say this," Jasper said with one paw over his nose, "but that is a sweet, sweet stink." The tree wobbled, let out a great big moan, and toppled over.

The animals jumped into the air and cheered. But their moment of joy was just that: a moment. The good news was that the tree roots remained attached, keeping it secured to the ground. The bad news, however, was really, really bad.

The tree was so brittle that when it slammed to the ground, it split over the middle of the cliff. The animals fell deathly quiet.

They could not believe what had just happened. They were so close. Now what were they going to do? The tree would be far too dangerous to cross. Whoever tried was certain to fall right through.

"We need someone as light as a feather," Jasper said.

"Well, I guess that would be me," replied Plump the Pot-Bellied Opossum.

All the animals looked at each other and scratched their heads. Plump thought he was as skinny as a twig. Since there were no mirrors in the forest, he never knew his beach ball belly was really as big as a pig's.

"Jasper said the lightest, not the fattest," Mario said.

Plump turned around with steam fuming from his ears, and boy, did he let loose! "Fat! Who are you calling fat, you overblown moose?"

Mario and Plump had been at odds with one another ever since Mario ate Francine the Ferret's delicious wild berry pie at last year's LOA picnic. It was Plump's favorite kind of pie. He had been drooling about a slice all winter long.

He had overslept and was late for the picnic. He arrived to find Mario wiping away the last of the wild berry crumbs from the fur on his face. When Plump found out he had eaten the entire pie, he was as furious as a forest fire.

Although Francine had gone out of her way to make another pie for Plump, he refused to forgive Mario. True, Mario should not have gobbled down the whole pie, but to be fair, Plump was late to the picnic, and let's face it: Since Mario weighed in at 1200 pounds, a whole pie is kind of like a slice to a moose.

"All right, knock it off. If we're going to save Ranger Mike, we're going to have to work as a team," Jasper ordered.

John the Worm wiggled forward and volunteered. "I will go," he said. "Just wrap the note around me."

Perfect, the animals thought. John could squirm close to the tree so the wind wouldn't knock him off, and even better, he weighed less than most feathers. He certainly wouldn't fall through.

"There is a slight problem, though," John said, "We worms are blessed with good looks, not speed. It would take me six weeks to make that trip."

Once again the orphaned animals were smacked in the face with an obstacle.

When all hope seemed to really have been lost, a soft-spoken voice changed everything. "I'll do it," the voice said.

Tank looked all around. "Who said that?" He asked.

"Me. Down here." Everyone looked to the ground. The voice belonged to Steffi the Chipmunk.

Steffi was the lightest of the orphaned animals, but she also had a disability; she was born with only three legs. Steffi never let her disability hold her back. In fact, she'd won the gold medal for fastest tree climber at the Chipmunk Games a few years ago.

It was her finish in the chipmunk branch-balancing event, however, that gave the orphaned animals the feeling of "Hey, we can finally do this. We can help save Ranger Mike."

Branch balancing measured the strength of bravery in a chipmunk's heart. The idea was to see how far you could walk out onto a weak and wobbly branch before the fear of falling made you leap to a stronger one. Steffi easily won the event.

"I'm the only one who stands a chance of crossing without the tree tumbling down," she said.

"Thank you for volunteering," Annie replied, and she placed the note in Steffi's mouth.

“Ready?” Jasper asked.

“Yes,” she said. Each of the orphaned animals gave her a kiss and hug. “I’ll do my best,” she said and placed the note in her mouth.

CHAPTER 9
The Woodland Spirit

Another rumble of thunder echoed in the distance. Annie the Antelope could tell the Wind Dragon was getting closer. A raindrop splashed down upon her nose. She glanced up, worried. The wind was bad enough, but rain was definitely something Steffi did not need. If it started to come down heavily, she would have to turn around and wait for it to stop. The old redwood tree would be too slippery to cross, even for Steffi.

Annie also knew, as she searched the sky for more raindrops, it would mean the end of the rescue. It could take the rest of the day for the redwood tree to dry.

Another raindrop fell; this time it landed in her eye. She wiped the water away with the back of her paw.

"As long as there are only a few raindrops, Steffi will be okay," Jasper the Coyote said to her. Annie did not seem to be listening to him. "Annie? Are you okay?" Jasper asked.

She was staring into the sky as if she were frozen in time. Suddenly, the other orphaned animals walked over to Annie; they too were looking into the sky. "What is so fascinating?" Jasper wondered. He looked up and paused in mid-thought. "Oh my," he said.

Out of the sky floated a green oak leaf that had broken away from its branch. The animals looked at the leaf in awe. The leaf never left their sight they did not even blink. "Talk about perfect timing," said Jasper with a smile. Though it might have looked like an ordinary oak leaf, it was not. It was a summer oak leaf that had fallen on its own, and that made all the difference in the world.

There is an old superstition among the animals in the forest, which goes something like this:

In the summertime
When you see an oak leaf fall from a tree
Close your eyes and count to three
Make a wish
Then reopen your eyes and say . . .
I believe . . . I believe . . . I believe . . .
And if you do
Your wish will come true
That is a promise, from the forest to you.

The orphaned animals could have very easily wished for something that would make their lives more comfortable, like enough food for the winter, or shelter to protect them from the Wind Dragon, or even to be reunited with their families. At this moment, however, none of that mattered. There was only one thing worth wishing for: Steffi's safe return home.

Just as she did when she inched out on the branch during the Squirrel Games, Steffi had one thought on her mind as she made her way over the cliff: "Don't look down," she said to herself over and over again. She had more courage in the tip of her tail than most animals had in their whole bodies. She would need every ounce of that courage to make it safely across.

When she reached the middle of the redwood, it became quite clear to her that she would have to go against her own advice and look down. The tree had splintered so badly that one missed step could be her last.

"Steffi? Are you okay?" Annie asked.

"Just dandy," she replied with a bit of humor, trying to calm their nerves. In truth, however, she was far from okay. There was nothing but air below her three claws. She took a deep breath. "I can do this," she whispered and edged her way across the splintered wood. The wood crackled and creaked with each step. "I can do this. I can do this," she repeated over and over in her head.

Finally, after what seemed like an eternity, she took one last step and breathed a sigh of relief, as did all her animal friends. Steffi had made it safely past the most dangerous portion of the redwood. It was clear sailing now.

"Yes!" Jasper said. The animals were elated. "Way to go, Steffi!" They cheered.

Steffi looked back, smiled and gave her friends a wave. All looked hopeful. Or so the animals thought.

The forest was a beautiful place, a land of fantasy and dreams, but it was also very unpredictable, and the animals were taught from birth not to take it for granted. Though the Wind Dragon had yet to show its evil red eye, it was about to make its presence known in the worst way possible.

The dark skies opened up, and rain began pouring down. "Hang on!" Jasper shouted to Steffi as he and the others raced to the edge of the cliff.

The rain was followed by a blast of thunder so powerful it shook the ground below the animals' paws. Steffi dug her claws into the tree bark to keep from falling over the edge. When the tree calmed, Steffi saw her chance. She released her grip and made a mad dash for the other side of the cliff. Her little paws, however, could not outrun the dragon's fury.

A lightning bolt exploded out of the clouds, striking the oak tree and setting it ablaze. Out of the fiery explosion of timber appeared an enormous tree branch twisting and twirling toward the ground. "Duck! Duck!" Annie shouted.

The branch passed harmlessly by. "That was a close one," Jasper said. Sadly, Steffi did not fare as well. The branch crashed down upon the splintered redwood tree, completely splitting it in half.

The rooted part of the tree stayed intact, but the end Steffi was on started to fall, "Help!" She shouted, but there was nothing her friends could do.

All the cheers and happiness gave way to sorrow. Everyone turned away and started to cry as the redwood tree disappeared down the cliff. They could not believe their friend was gone.

Annie opened her eyes and watched the oak leaf that had given them so much hope touch down on the ground in front of her. The edges of the leaf began to turn brown and crinkle. "I'll miss you so much, Steffi," she said, wiping away her tears with her paw.

"A little help," whispered a voice.

Mario looked up. "It's as if I can hear little Steffi's spirit," he said as he whimpered.

"A little help," the voice whispered once more.

Annie's eyes opened wide. "What in the world?" She said. The dying oak leaf started to come back to life. The ends unwrinkled, and it once again turned bright green. "Wait a minute," she said as the voice was heard for a third time. "That is not Steffi's spirit." She raced over to the edge of the cliff and looked out. "Steffi!"

She said with delight, "you're alive!" All the other animals raced over to Annie's side.

Steffi was dangling by a single claw from the bottom of the redwood tree. "Please hurry. I can't hold on much longer," she said.

The animals looked around with panic in their eyes. "What do we do? What do we do?" They all shouted.

"I've got this one," said Plump the Opossum. "Everyone out of the way."

"Not a chance," said Annie. "The tree will never hold you."

Plump turned to his fellow animals. "Look," he said. "I know I'm not the skinniest animal in the forest. I don't need a mirror to figure that out, but my tail is the only one long enough to reach Steffi."

Though everyone agreed with Annie, they knew Plump was right. He was Steffi's only hope.

Plump took a deep breath and climbed onto the old redwood. "Just don't look down," Steffi said.

"That will not be a problem," Plump replied with a nervous chuckle. He slowly turned around and carefully backed his way over the edge of the cliff.

As he did, the wind miraculously died down and the rain slowed to a sprinkle. The old redwood itself didn't seem to present much of a problem. It creaked with each step, but never once did Plump feel as if it were about to give way.

Feeling more confident, Plump picked up his pace. The animals on land saw the confidence in Plump's eyes, and they too began to relax a bit. They were as sure as sure could be: nothing was going to stop Plump from rescuing Steffi.

Mario the Moose, however, realized, out of the corner of his eye, just why you should never take the forest for granted.

The roots, holding the tree to the ground, were snapping like twigs. No one noticed because all eyes were glued on Plump's every step. The faster Plump stepped, the faster the roots snapped.

"Yikes!" Mario said. He quickly turned to Plump. "Slow down!"

Plump and all the animals looked over to Mario as he weaved his way through the animals in front of him. Mario lunged for the tree as the last root gave way, and he snatched it out of midair with his teeth. The tree stump jerked down. Plump dropped his belly and held on for dear life.

"I got it!" Mario grunted, as he steadied the tree. He then pulled back his head, dug his hooves into the muddy ground, and held on with all his might.

Mario's grip was the only thing stopping Plump and Steffi from tumbling down the side of the cliff with the tree.

There was the problem. Though a moose's body was mighty strong, its teeth were not. In fact, a moose didn't even have upper front teeth. Mario had to hold the entire tree trunk from falling with just his lower teeth and upper gums.

It would take every last bit of determination in his body to hold on.

"Go! Go!" The animals shouted. Mario nodded to Plump, as if to say, "I won't let you down."

Plump lifted up his belly and quickly moon-danced his way down the tree trunk, his stomach swaying from side to side. When he reached the end of the tree, he flopped his tail down to Steffi. Steffi closed her eyes and took the leap of faith. "Yes!" She said as she snagged his tail.

Plump whipped his tail upward, tossing Steffi into the air. She did a double back flip with a twist and landed securely on his back. "Let's ride!" She yelled as she dug her claws into his fur.

Plump lowered his head and made a run for it.

The root in Mario's mouth began to break apart. Annie realized they weren't going to make it. "Leap for the edge!" She shouted. The root gave way and Mario tumbled over backwards. When he looked up again, he was met with his worst fear: The old redwood had disappeared down the side of the cliff, and a fifty-pound pot-bellied opossum was flying through the air.

"Oh no!" Mario said, slapping his cheeks. Plump's front paws were able to reach land, but his back paws fell short and dangled over the edge. "No worries," Jasper said. "We gotcha." Jasper and Tank the Buffalo each grabbed a paw and pulled Plump and Steffi to safety.

Everyone smothered Steffi and Plump and Mario with hugs and kisses. "What do you say we give them the mighty forest cheer," said Tank. "ROAR! ROAR! ROARRRR!"

Annie walked over to Steffi. "This is for you, Steffi," she said, and handed her the oak leaf.

"Thank you," Steffi replied.

"Though it is only a silly superstition, I'm so happy our wish came true," Annie said.

"Not as happy as I am," Steffi replied. All the animals laughed.

Annie then turned to Plump and gave him a hug. "Sorry I doubted you," she said. "We all are."

"It's okay," Plump replied. "I don't blame you. Like I said, I know I'm not the skinniest animal here. I'm just glad I could help."

Suddenly, Plump felt a shadow creep over him. He slowly turned around and looked up. Mario was staring him down.

"Easy now, boys," Jasper said.

"Nice work, chunky," said Mario.

"You, too, lughead," Plump replied. They both broke out with smiles and gave each other a hoof tap.

Mario and Plump may not have been the best of friends, but that didn't matter at the moment. As Jasper said, they were a team and a pretty darn good one at that.

"I hate to burst everyone's bubble, guys, but not all is peachy keen," said Rollo the Monarch Butterfly.

They all gathered at the edge of the cliff. "Oh no!" Said Annie. "The note!" In all the commotion, they totally forgot about the note. It was floating aimlessly down the side of the cliff. "I can't believe it!" Jasper said.

"It will take a miracle to save Ranger Mike now," Zelda said.

Little did Zelda and her friends know that the miracle was about to take place. A whirling tail of light appeared from the depths of the cliff, and beautiful music filled the air. "It's the Wind Dragon! It's going to suck us all down the cliff," Plump said.

The animals gathered closely together, hugging each other tight, all shivering with fright. That was until they heard a gentle voice. "There is no need to be afraid," it said.

The tail of the light twirled before their eyes and exploded, raining silver and blue stars down upon their heads.

Out of the light appeared Nia the Woodland Spirit. The animals were absolutely mesmerized. "Oh my! She does exist!" Annie whispered in awe.

Nia appeared in human form, as beautiful as an angel. She had long, silky brown hair, beautiful indigo-colored eyes, and a smile that could warm the coldest heart.

The animals relaxed and watched as Nia swooped down upon the note. With a gentle twirl of her finger, the note changed course. It floated up toward the sky and landed ever so gently on the other side of the cliff.

Nia flapped her white, fluorescent wings and floated before the orphaned animals. She smiled and looked toward Zelda. "Always remember and never forget," she said, "the love in your heart, Zelda, the love in all your hearts, is more precious than a thousand miracles." Nia then nodded good-bye and faded into the wind.

CHAPTER 10
A Stinky Situation

Ollie the Weasel and his brother Wart arrived home with branches and twigs to help secure their family burrow. Ollie could not stop thinking about his encounter with Tombstone. He was so upset, his belly was twisted in knots.

Wart patted him on the back. "There was nothing we could do, big brother," he said. "It is best, for the sake of our family, to just forget it ever happened."

"I should have stood up to him," Ollie said to himself. "Instead I just ran away like a coward. Because of me, Ranger Mike might never be saved."

He knew he couldn't just bury the secret in his fur. Even though he knew Tombstone would eat him for lunch if he found out he snitched, he had to do something. "I have to let Ricky know," he thought. "I just have to."

"Ollie," his dad cried out. "We still need a few more branches."

"Oh, okay," Ollie replied. "I'll be right back," he said.

This was his chance. He quickly made his way through the tall grass and over to Ricky's house. Ollie spotted Ricky and yelled out his name.

"Hey, Ollie," he said, "what's up?"

"I have some bad news." Ricky waddled over to him. "What's the matter, Ollie?" He asked.

Ollie shamefully explained to him what had happened. "Tombstone threatened my family if we squealed. I don't know if I'm doing the right thing. I just know I had to tell someone."

Ricky felt really bad for Ollie. "You did the only thing you could do, Ollie. None of us can stand up to Tombstone. Like Merlin said, he is a bully."

Ollie turned, picked up a few branches that had fallen due to the wind, and moped his way back home.

Ricky stood there in the rain, pondering what to do. Shelby scooted from her tree nest and joined Ricky in the rain. She'd heard everything Ollie had said. "The Wind Dragon is going to be here in no time. We have to try and get the phone back, Ricky. It might be our only chance."

"You're right," Ricky said, "but how?"

"Mountain lions sleep during the day and hunt at night. Maybe we can sneak into Tombstone's lair and take it while he is sleeping."

"That might work," Ricky replied. He then looked up into the sky. The rain was pouring down and the thunder was drawing closer. "We'll have to go now," he said. Shelby took a deep breath and nodded yes.

Ricky and Shelby looked back at their homes. They thought about their brothers, sisters, mom and dad, and all the good times they'd had over the years.

"We'll be okay," Ricky said.

"I know we will," Shelby replied as she stored a few nuts in her mouth for the journey.

Deep down, however, they both realized there was a good chance they would never return.

Ricky took a deep breath. "Let's do this," he said, and they set out to find Tombstone's lair.

Meanwhile, on a brighter note, it did not take long for the Land of Orphaned Animals to receive good news. A beautiful red fox named Lauren wandered by on the other side of the cliff. "Hey!" "Help!" "Over here!" the animals yelled out, waving their paws in the air.

Lauren stepped ever so ladylike to the edge of the cliff. Plump couldn't believe his eyes. "Wow!" He said as his jaw practically dropped to the ground. "She's a looker!"

"Oh, you got that right," replied Mario. "As fine as a blueberry vine."

Hilda the Hedgehog turned and looked at Plump and Mario. "Oh brother," she said with disgust and a shake of her head.

Lauren ignored everyone else and looked straight into Jasper's big brown eyes. "Hi there, handsome," she said with a flirty smile.

Jasper froze. He didn't know what to say. And even if he did, it would have been useless; he was so nervous he couldn't move his lips.

"Come on," Annie said out of the corner of her mouth. "Put on your charm. Tell her about the note."

"Note, ground," he muttered.

Annie rolled her eyes. "Real smooth," she remarked.

Lauren looked to the ground and lifted the note. "Jasper has a sore throat," Annie said, making an excuse for his twisted tongue.

"What he wanted to say is... will you please bring the note to the farmhouse? One of the forest rangers is hurt real badly and in need of our help." She went on to explain Operation Friendship.

"I see, I see," Lauren replied, never taking her eyes off Jasper. "Well, anything for you, handsome," she said and took a step away from the cliff. She then turned and looked at Jasper one last time. "Bye-bye, sweetie pie," she said and blew him a kiss.

Jasper wanted to come back with a cool response like "Thanks, babe" or "Catch you later, baby doll," but he was so nervous all he could muster were the words, "Yeah, okay, yeah."

"Way to go, Casanova," Annie said jokingly.

Lauren made her way down a small hill to a short wooden fence that surrounded a great big farmhouse painted white with red trim. Milk cows were feeding in the pasture, and baby sheep were running around and playing.

"I'll drop the note at the door and ring the bell," she thought. "That will do the trick." She ducked under the fence and was met by two bulging black eyeballs. "Yikes!" She yelled out and leaped back.

Staring her down on the other side of the fence was a Rottweiler named Bones. Bones had one purpose in life: to keep all vermin out of the farmyard.

His looks alone were enough to scare away even the most determined trespassers. He had scars all over his face, drool was dripping from his mouth, and he had a tattoo on his right front leg that read "I'm Just Plain Mean."

Lauren took a step forward, and Bones lifted his upper lip and growled. "Seriously," she said, "listen, fella, I really don't have time for this. I need to get this note to the Ranger Station. I'm already late for my hair appointment. So step aside and let a lady pass."

She took another step forward, but Bones wasn't offering up any goodwill on this day. He snapped at her and snorted wetly.

Lauren leaped back. "Ouch!" She yelled, smacking her paw on a rock. "Look at what you did!" She said in anger. "You made me break a claw." The one thing you did not want to do was get Lauren angry. "That's it, snot breath! If you think you can keep me from crossing this yard, you are in for a big surprise, pal. No animal, and I mean no animal, outfoxes this chick," Lauren said and stormed away.

Bones wasn't the least bit impressed. He sat down on his hind legs, folded his front paws, and snickered at Lauren, as if to say, "I'm real scared, princess."

Lauren stomped behind a large boulder, anger fuming from her ears. "I have to do something," she said, "but what?" Just then she noticed a number of mole holes and a family of skunks chowing down on a delicious slug salad. Her body calmed and a smile replaced her frown. She had an idea, and a rather clever one at that.

Bones was still sitting at the fence with his front paws folded when Lauren approached him again. "Well, my friend. Being that I am a lady, I will give you one last chance to be a nice little doggie and let me pass by." "You've got to be kidding me," Bones grumbled and broke out in laughter.

Lauren glanced past Bones and watched as three mole heads popped out of the ground directly behind him. Bones was laughing so hard, he never heard them. The moles gave Lauren the paws up, and they ducked back underground.

"Okay," she said. "Never let it be said I didn't give you a chance."

Suddenly, Bones stopped laughing, and his face turned white as a ghost. "Uh-oh!" He said as he took a few whiffs.

"I would like you to meet a few of my new friends," Lauren said. Bones slowly turned around. Staring up at him, in front of the mole holes, stood three of the most feared creatures in the forest.

"Introducing the Skunk Brothers: Smelly, Stinky, and Stench."

Bones laughed nervously through his quivering lips. "Fellas," he said, "I'm sure we could talk this out."

Lauren ducked under the fence and walked past Bones. "Like I said, no one outfoxes this chick," and she gave the Skunk Brothers a wink.

Smelly, Stinky, and Stench spun around, raised their tails, aimed, and sprayed away.

"Ahhhhhhhhh!" Bones yelled out. He leaped over the skunk brothers, zipped past Lauren, and made a beeline for the pigsty. "Outta my way!" He shouted, hoping a mud bath would subdue the smell. He knocked over a pig named Pug and did a header into the mud. The smell was so nasty, even the pigs couldn't deal with it. "P.U., man," Pug said as he lifted himself up. "Get your stink out of here!" Pug, along with a few of his friends, lifted Bones up, flung him out of their pen, and he landed face first in a humongous pile of cow manure. Which, ironically, smelled like a bed of roses compared to the skunk odor.

Lauren put a little giddy-up into her step as she crossed the farmyard. She wasn't afraid Bones would seek revenge; a five-ton elephant had a better chance of sneaking up on her, but rather she was super late for her hair appointment. "There," she said, noticing a farm stand. "I'll just casually drop off the note."

She walked around to the front of the stand, "Oh rats!" She said in frustration. "I can't believe it." A sign posted on the stand read "Closed – On Vacation."

"How do, ma'am," said a chunky calico cat relaxing on top

of a fifty-gallon pickle barrel. "The name is Big Stanley," he said with a tip of his cowboy hat. "What seems to be the problem?"

"I need to get this note to the Ranger Station, but I don't know where it is. A ranger is hurt real bad."

"Well, ma'am, you're in luck. The Ranger Station is just down yonder," he said, pointing to a rocky dirt road.

"Oh," Lauren replied. She had already broken one claw; the dirt road would create havoc on her pampered paws.

"Can you do me a really big super-duper favor and please take the note for me?" She asked with pouty eyes. "I'm afraid I will get lost. Can you please?"

No male animal, outside of Bones that is, could ever resist Lauren's charm.

"Why, it would be my pleasure ma'am," he said.

"Thanks, darling," she replied and gave him a peck on the cheek.

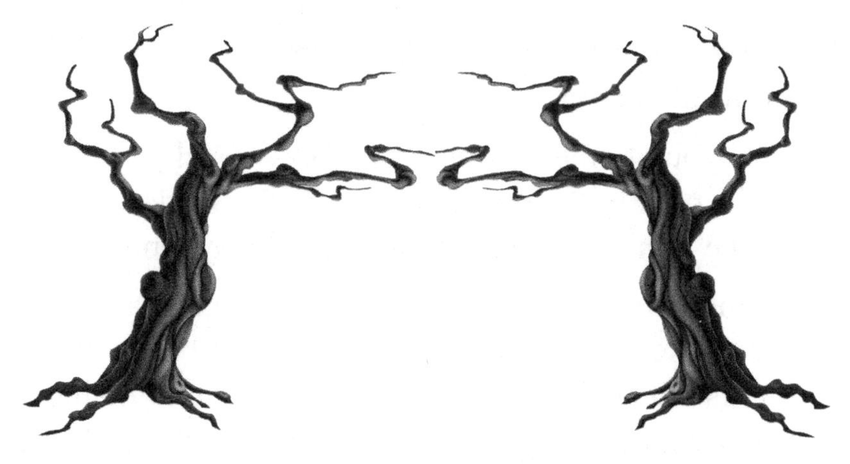

CHAPTER 11
Samp Mortar Swamp

Shelby and Ricky had no way of knowing the Ranger Station was now within reach. They had only one thought on their minds: to do whatever it took to get the cell phone back from Tombstone.

The storm was getting more dangerous with each step through the forest. As they approached the foot of Mount Chubaluba, Ricky began thinking about the whole scenario concerning the Wind Dragon. Something just didn't make sense to him.

"Shelby," he said, as he stopped, "this isn't right."

"What do you mean, Ricky?" Shelby asked.

"Think about it. Why would a powerful Wind Dragon threaten to destroy an entire forest just because of name-calling? There has to be more to the story."

"I've been thinking the same thing, Ricky. Maybe this is just another storm. Since no one has ever really seen the Wind Dragon, maybe, just maybe, it doesn't exist at all. It could simply be a figment of our imagination."

At that moment, dark, menacing clouds consumed the sky, leaving the forest just like a hundred years ago, pitch black, as if it were the dead of night.

"I think your figment spoke too soon," Ricky said, as he looked to the peak of the mountain. Out of the shadows crept the red eye of the Wind Dragon. "I think so," Shelby replied.

The Wind Dragon latched its skeleton-like claws around the mountain, let out a thundering growl, and shot lightning bolts from its wings like laser beams. One of the lightning bolts struck the ground just a few feet away from Ricky and Shelby. The forest floor began to crack open as if it were a sheet of ice. The cracks slithered toward Shelby and Ricky like angry rattlesnakes. Before Ricky and Shelby could make a run for it, the ground below their feet opened up, and they fell through a crack.

"What's happening?" Shelby screamed.

"I don't know! Just hang on!" Ricky said, and he reached out and grabbed her paw.

They were plowing through the earth as if they were on an underground rollercoaster. If it weren't for the fact that they had no idea where they were going, it would have actually been a pretty cool ride.

They came around a bend at an incredible rate of speed. "Pull back!" Ricky shouted. There was a boulder in front of them. They both leaned backwards and their bodies lifted upwards, clearing the boulder by the fur on their backs.

"Close!" Ricky said.

"Too close," Shelby replied. "I want to get off!"

Ricky looked up. "I think you are about to get your wish," he said.

They splashed through the bottom of a mud puddle and

tumbled out into a dark and eerie mist. Shelby quietly sat up and shook the water from her fur. "Are you okay, Ricky?"

"Yes," Ricky replied, and he did the same.

The mist was so thick they could barely see two feet in front of them.

"Are we where I think we are?" Shelby whispered.

"I'm afraid so, Shelby," Ricky replied. "Samp Mortar Swamp."

They slowly moved forward through the ghostly mist. Every crackle of a leaf and snap of a twig sent shivers down their spines. It was like walking through a graveyard at the toll of midnight, never knowing when the creeps would come out to play.

"I'm scared, Ricky," Shelby said.

"Me too, Shelby."

Suddenly, they felt a warm, gentle breeze across the side of their fur, as if someone or something was breathing on them. They came to a dead stop and slowly turned to their left.

Hovering over them was an old, wrinkled tree with claw-like branches. Though the tree looked dead, make no mistake, it was very much alive. A face with jagged scars was carved into the bark. Its eyes were closed, and a whimpering sound flowed from the edge of its mouth.

"Shhhh," Shelby said. "It's sleeping."

Shelby and Ricky backed slowly away, trying their hardest not to make a sound. Ricky accidentally stumbled over one of the tree's vines protruding from the ground. The tree immediately awoke with a ferocious roar, its bloodshot eyes staring down at Ricky and Shelby.

"Who dares enter into the mist?" The tree said wickedly.

"We mean no harm," Shelby replied as she huddled close to Ricky.

"Well, unfortunately for you, I do."

The tree lashed out at them with its claw-like branches. Flowers rose out of the ground and tried to sting them with their poisonous petals. Ricky and Shelby danced their way around the attack, until a weed wrapped itself around Shelby's leg. Ricky did not hesitate. Raccoons had a mighty bite. He latched onto the weed and ripped it off her leg.

"Let's get out of here!" He said, and they booked.

"Look, Ricky! Up ahead. I think I see a light," Shelby said.

Ricky slowed down to catch his breath, "I see it too, Shelby. It has to be the way out."

"Let's go," Shelby said.

Ricky took a few steps and stopped. "Wait, Shelby! It's a trap!" Ricky yelled out. Raccoons had very sensitive front paws. He felt the temperature of the ground rise dramatically. Shelby stopped, and she was very lucky she did.

Ricky pulled away some branches and weeds, revealing a body of murky swamp water covered in moss and lily pads. Steam was rising out of the water.

"Whatever lives in the water put these here to fool its prey," he whispered. He picked up a twig and tossed it into the water. The twig instantly ignited and turned to ash.

"That water has to be a gazillion degrees," Shelby said. "What do we do now?"

"Well," Ricky replied, "whatever it is, we'd better do it and fast. Look!" Something was crawling toward them through the grass. They looked at each other. "COCKROACHES!" They shouted. Without hesitation, they kicked back their tails and did the only thing they could: the lily pad leap.

Shelby was lighter on her paws than Ricky and had no problem making it safely across the boiling swamp water. “Hurry, Ricky, hurry!” Shelby yelled as she dug her paws into the cool mud to soothe them from the heat.

“I’m trying!” Ricky replied.

About halfway across, Shelby lifted her front paws out of the mud and slapped her cheeks. “Watch out!” She screamed.

Out of the water launched two of the most feared insect predators known to man: giant, grotesque water bugs. Similar to the black widow spider, they were known for drinking their prey.

Ricky ducked just in time; the water bugs slammed heads and exploded into a ball of fire. Before Ricky could make another move, the head of a giant rat splashed out of the water and bobbed up and down in front of him. Ricky froze and then let out a sigh as the rat head fell off to the side. “Wow, that was close,” Ricky said. It was obvious, by its chewed and mangled body, that the rat had fallen for the water bugs’ trap and had become their lunch. “It’s dead,” Ricky said.

Or was it?

The rat’s eyes flashed open. It righted its head, snarled, and launched at Ricky with its razor-sharp teeth. Ricky’s survival instincts kicked in. He flipped through the air and somersaulted over the rat’s head, landing paws first on a lily pad.

The water bugs quickly swarmed all around him. Ricky wasn’t about to become a victim of their feeding frenzy. He took a deep breath and leaped with all his might, landing safely in Shelby’s arms.

“That was way too close!” Ricky said. “Let’s get the H-E-double bamboo sticks out of here!”

“No argument from me,” Shelby replied. “This place is creep city!”

The creatures in Samp Mortar Swamp, however, were not about to let such tasty and delectable treats simply walk free.

Two nasty-looking horseflies with bulging black eyes the size of basketballs rose from the tall grass, blocking their path to the light. "You have got to be kidding me!" Ricky said. They looked frantically for another way to escape.

"There!" Ricky shouted, pointing to the left. "That looks like a hill! We can climb it to safety!" Ricky was banking on the idea that the mutated insects could only survive in the mist. Once outside, they would return to their normal shape and size, thus becoming harmless.

Shelby and Ricky made a mad dash for the hill. As they approached the hill, it became more and more apparent that it wasn't what they thought. Instead of a hill, it was a mangled pile of metal.

"Wait a minute, Ricky," Shelby said. "What is it?'

"I think it's Ranger Mike's plane," Ricky replied, as a chill raced down his spine. It was quite an eerie sight.

"Ranger Mike was lucky he had that parachute," Shelby said.

"Yeah," Ricky replied. "And so are we."

Shelby glanced back over her shoulder. "Hurry," she said. The flies were gaining on them. They climbed what remained of the left wing, leaped up to the roof and out across the right wing, the tip of which, thankfully, lifted out of the swamp. "That was so beyond close," Shelby said as she and Ricky held onto each other to keep from falling off the wing. The mist from the swamp made the wing quite slippery.

"Wowza, you're not kidding, Shelby," Ricky replied.

One of the flies was not as lucky. It was so eager to capture its prey, it forgot to stop, and made the grave mistake of following Shelby and Ricky out of the mist.

The fly lifted its wings in victory as it buzzed in front of Ricky and Shelby's eyes. It figured a mighty feast was about to take place. That was until the fly caught a glimpse of its wings and realized it had made a big mistake. "Oops! Just kidding," it whispered. "Forget you ever saw me." The fly started to whistle and gently back its way toward the mist, hoping not to draw any attention. Unfortunately, in the forest, much like in the swamp, a possible meal never goes unnoticed.

"Hey, pal," a voice grumbled. The fly slowly turned his head. "Oh, momma," it said. A chameleon lashed out its tongue and slurped him down. "That hit the spot!" It said and burped.

"Where do we go from here?" Shelby asked. "We can't hang on forever."

"Up here, guys," replied a voice. Shelby and Ricky looked up. A tree snake named Butchy was dangling from a branch. "Climb up, my friends, and I will form a snake rope from tree to tree and will zip line you to safety."

"Awesome deal," Ricky said.

Ricky and Shelby wrapped their front claws around the snake line to form a latch. "Ready?" Ricky asked. Shelby looked down. Not knowing what circled in the mist below was more terrifying than the bottomless pit.

"As I'll ever be," she replied.

They gave Butchy a nod, kicked off with their hind legs, and glided down the zip line. It looked like the perfect plan. What could possibly go wrong? There was nothing between them and their freedom but the wind blowing through their fur.

That was until a branch holding the zip line in place snapped just as Shelby was swinging by. The zip line jerked downward and Shelby lost her balance for a brief moment; her dangling paw grazed the top of the mist. That tiny mistake was all the swamp creatures needed. They jumped at the opportunity and snagged her leg.

"Ricky!" Shelby yelled out. Ricky had already reached the next tree. He quickly swung around. "No!" He yelled out. Shelby was barely hanging on. Ricky felt hopeless; there was nothing he could do to help.

They stared into each other's eyes. "Go, Ricky," Shelby whispered. "Save yourself." She then closed her eyes and was pulled into the mist. Ricky turned away. Even though Shelby wanted him to continue on without her, there was no way he was about to leave his friend behind. His sadness quickly turned to anger and then to determination. "We started this adventure together. We'll finish it together, Shelby," he said. "Friends together! Friends forever!"

He then glanced up at Butchy. "Thanks for helping," he said, took a deep breath, and let go.

CHAPTER 12
Double Trouble

Big Stanley the Cat jumped through a wooden fence and trotted over to the dirt road. He looked both ways. There were no cars in sight, so he began crossing the road. What he failed to notice, however, was the road sign right next to him, which read ATV DUNE BUGGY RACE TODAY!

Halfway across the road, a bright light flashed through the corner of his eye. Big Stanley turned to his left. “BEEP! BEEP!” Blasted a horn.

“Get out of the road, cat!” “BEEP! BEEP!” Big Stanley scrambled to his left and then to the right, dodging the dune buggies as they zoomed by. “BEEP! BEEP!” Back to his left and again to his right. Eight of his nine lives passed before his eyes. “BEEP! BEEP!” “Oh no,” he said. The last-place dune buggy was heading right for him. He froze like a deer in the headlights, expecting to become fender food. Miraculously, the dune buggy hit a bump in the road and flew over him.

"All right!" Big Stanley shouted with delight, followed by an "Uh-oh." He caught his tail on the dune buggy's back fender.

"There goes life number nine," he said, and was jerked off the ground and launched down the road so fast he left his fur behind.

A beautiful white-tailed deer named Kristen was feeding on roadside grass when Big Stanley streaked by. "Liiiiiiiiiittle heeeeeeeelp!" He shouted and disappeared down the road. Kristen looked up and paused. "Did I just see what I thought I saw?"

"Oh, you did indeed," said her friend Jessamyn the Marmot as she popped her head out of her burrow. "A fat, bald cat, wearing a cowboy hat."

"What is this, Jess?" Kristen wondered. Big Stanley lost control of the note as he passed by, and it floated gently to the ground in front of Kristen.

The second she read what it said, her heart began to thump. "This is terrible," she said. No animals in the forest depended on a ranger more than deer.

Even though NO HUNTING! Signs were posted throughout the forest, it did little to stop the humans from doing so. The worst culprit was Harley the Hunter. He simply refused to obey the law of the land.

Kristen was about to find out just how little he thought of the laws. Harley quietly stepped between two trees and snickered as he raised his bow and arrow toward Kristen. "Gonna get me sum suppa," he said, and pulled back on the arrow string.

Kristen was in trouble, but it was no day at the beach for Ricky either. He fell through the mist and bounced off the head of a giant red fire ant. Before the ant could make a move, Ricky grabbed its antennae. "Sorry, bud, but I don't have time for this." He stretched the ant's antennae as if they were rubber bands, and let go. The antennae sprang forward and smacked the poor fellow right in the mush.

The ant's senses were out of whack. "I'll you get?" He repeated over and over again while running around in circles.

"That should hold him for a while," Ricky said, and moved cautiously through the swamp in search of Shelby. He climbed to the top of a hill and peeked over. Through the mist he spotted Shelby in the distance, held captive by a praying mantis named Dredd.

Outside the mist, a praying mantis was harmless to most animals. Inside the mist, however, it was as feared as a tyrannosaurus rex. A sickening thought tightened Ricky's belly, and he knew he had to act fast. According to his encyclopedia, a praying mantis subdues its prey by biting off their heads.

He ran down the hill as fast as he could, waving his paws in the air, trying to draw Dredd's attention away from Shelby. Shelby could not believe her eyes.

"Ricky?" She said. She'd never expected to see her best friend again. "Don't come any closer," she warned.

"It's okay. He won't harm me," he replied. Ricky was right. Praying mantises were patient hunters. They waited in the shadows for their prey to find them. Dredd was not about to give up his meal ticket to chase after Ricky.

Shelby tried to squirm free, but Dredd's spiked forelegs made it impossible. It was like trying to fight your way out of a rose bush.

Ricky searched high and low for an idea. "What do I do? What do I do? Come on. Think! There has to be something I can do," he said.

Shelby stopped her squirming. "Ricky," she said and rolled an acorn out on her tongue. Ricky knew exactly what she meant.

"Oh yeah! Batting practice!" He said.

Shelby and Ricky had met while playing on the same acorn league team, the Chubaluba Tree Dwellers. The acorn league was similar to baseball, only instead of a wooden bat and cowhide ball, they used a bamboo stick and an acorn wrapped in shed snakeskin.

Ricky was the team's best hitter and Shelby the team's best pitcher.

Ricky grabbed a branch from the ground, stood up on his hind legs, and raised the branch over his shoulder. "Give me one right down the middle," he said.

Shelby took a deep breath and spit the acorn toward him. Ricky swung and the acorn blasted off the branch and nailed Dredd in the left arm. He lost his grip, and his arm fell off to the side.

Shelby spit a second acorn out. Ricky waited till the last second and ripped another line drive, this time off Dredd's right arm. It too went numb and fell to his side.

Shelby was free from Dredd's clutches, but she knew if she took one step forward, he would snatch her in his mouth. "One more, Shelby, and this time with a little juice," Ricky encouraged. With her arms now free, Shelby spit the acorn into her paw, wound up, and threw a heater right down the middle. Ricky cocked the branch back and swung with all his might. The acorn exploded off the branch and beaned Dredd right off the forehead.

Dredd's legs began to wobble. "A, B, C you later," Ricky said, and Dredd fell face first into the swamp, out cold.

Shelby stepped over Dredd and gave Ricky a hug. "We'd better get out of here before he wakes up," Ricky said. And there was an even more pressing reason to hightail it. The noise created when Dredd hit the ground woke every insect in the swamp.

Mosquitoes, slugs, ants, beetles, termites, cockroaches, and yes, even butterflies began their attack.

"Where to, Ricky?" Shelby asked.

"There! The light!" Ricky replied.

"But it's useless, Ricky. We'll never make it," Shelby said, and she was right. The swarms of insects were practically on top of them.

As luck would have it, two dragonflies the size of eagles flew out in front of Ricky and Shelby on the prowl for food. Dragonflies had no ears, so they couldn't hear all the commotion behind them. Even better, Ricky knew from reading his encyclopedia, dragonflies were among the fastest insects in the world.

Ricky turned toward the swarm of insects and gave them a salute. "Love to stay and chat, fellas, but we have a flight to catch."

Ricky and Shelby ran up and leaped onto the backs of the dragonflies. After catching their balance, the dragonflies shifted their eyes and snapped at Ricky and Shelby with their deadly mandibles. Before they could go in for the kill, Ricky pointed over his shoulder. The dragonflies' big eyes bulged open wide. Would the army of insects be content to eat only the animals? Or would they too become prey? The dragonflies were not about to stick around and find out.

They flapped their wings and left the insects in their dust. "Smooth sailing now," Ricky said as they blazed a trail toward the light.

"I don't know about you, Ricky, but winter hibernation can't come fast enough for me," Shelby replied.

Upon entering the light, something strange began to happen. The light flickered, dimmed, and went dark altogether. “I have a bad feeling about this,” Shelby said.

In the distance, Ricky noticed something or someone, and as the figure crept closer, he realized Shelby’s instincts were right on target. The light was not safe passage to the outside. “Make a leap for it, Shelby!” Ricky yelled. “It’s the Wind Dragon!”

The all-too-familiar ferocious roar rocked the swamp floor, and the menacing red eye of the Wind Dragon opened wide, consuming everything in its path. Shelby and Ricky were able to jump free just in time. Unfortunately, the two dragonflies did not fare as well. They flew through the eye of the Wind Dragon and whirled into its belly like a goldfish down a toilet bowl.

Ricky and Shelby tumbled across the ground and staggered to their paws, but there was nowhere to run. The insects had surrounded them. “What do we do now, Ricky?” Shelby asked.

“I don’t know, Shelby,” Ricky replied.

Out of the pack stepped the fire ant Ricky had knocked for a loop. The ant lowered its bulbous, almost jelly-like head and snapped its sharp mandibles at Ricky.

“Friend of yours?” Shelby asked in jest.

“Not exactly,” he replied.

The fire ant stepped back and cleared a pathway. Down the aisle stomped Dredd with a big old welt on his head. Needless to say, he was not in a forgiving mood.

CHAPTER 13
Believe in the Magic

Harley the Hunter had a face only a mother could love: a dark scratchy beard, a very hairy nose, and skeleton eyes. It was obvious by his grin that he put very little stock into dental hygiene. Half of his teeth were missing, and half of the half he had were yellow and green.

Harley followed Kristen the White-Tailed Deer's every step through the forest with the point of his arrow. Kristen was so concerned about getting the note to the Ranger Station, she let down her guard. She had no clue that Harley had her in his sights. Luckily for her, Jessamyn the Marmot had her back.

Jessamyn and Kristen were best of friends and always looked out for each other. Kristen's keen sense of smell warned Jessamyn when a hawk was prowling above the neighborhood, and Jessamyn would act as a scout and make sure there were no hunters in the area.

"Gonna get me sum suppa," Harley grunted again. The forest was covered in thick redwood trees, but that didn't matter to Harley. "Ain't no tree gonna stop me," he said and let go.

The arrow was so powerful it exploded through the tree trunks, one after the other. Jess heard the noise and quickly turned just as the arrow blasted through the final redwood tree. "Kristen!" She shouted. "Duck!" Without hesitation, Kristen lowered her head. The arrow grazed her ear, ricocheted off a boulder, and sailed out of control.

Queen Bertha the Bumblebee had just put her finishing touches on the new hive. "Ahhh, it is a piece of art," she said with tears of joy, "Without that goofball Buford around, nothing could possibly threaten our new home. Thank you, everyone, for all your hard work." All the bees buzzed with joy.

Bertha then paused and listened. "Hmmm," she said. "What is that humming sound?"

"Your Majesty, look out!" Shouted a bee named Rosie. It was too late; the arrow whizzed past Bertha and sent her into a free fall. She flipped through the air and landed face first in the mud.

She dug herself out of the mud, wiped her wings clean, and slowly turned around, her stinger thumping with anger. The arrow had gone right through her brand-new hive, destroying every last bit of it.

Harley pulled out another arrow from his shoulder holster and stretched it back on the bow. Kristen was so scared she couldn't move. "No worries, girlfriend," said Queen Bertha as she flew by. "He's all mine."

Just like Ranger Mike had suggested, Mother Nature did come knocking on Harley's door, in the form of an angry swarm of bees.

Harley noticed the black wave coming his way, threw up his bow and arrow, and took off.

"I'll say one thing about Harley, Jess," Kristen said as she looked on. "For a chubby fella, he is pretty quick on his feet."

“Not quick enough,” Jess replied with a wince, as Bertha and her family caught up to him. “Ouch! That’s going to leave a mark.”

“Yeah,” Kristen agreed, “a thousand of them.”

After Bertha and her family completed their attack, Harley’s head swelled to the size of a beach ball, and his face resembled a rotten apple. “How perfect is that,” Kristen said.

It didn’t look like Ricky and Shelby were going to fare as well as Kristen. Dredd tied on his bib and rubbed his forearms together, ready to feast on a little payback. The fire ant stepped alongside Dredd. “You can have the leftovers,” Dredd said. “Now, off with their heads!”

All hope rushed out of Shelby and Ricky’s bodies, and they went limp. They simply had no more fight in them. Their fate had been sealed. They felt they would be doomed to the hollows of Dredd’s belly for eternity.

Dredd lifted up his forearm and took a swipe at Shelby and Ricky, but came away with nothing but air. The ground below their feet cracked open once again, and to their surprise, they were sent on another rollercoaster ride through the earth.

Given the fact that they’d been a second away from becoming mantis meat, this time the ride was a welcome one. That was, until they came around a bend and found themselves staring down the same boulder they’d encountered in the last go-around.

“You have got to be kidding me!” Shelby said. “We’re right back where we started. What is this, some kind of a crazy maze?”

“I don’t know,” Ricky replied. “Just hang on tight.”

They leaned back and cleared the rock by the fur on their backs. Instead of launching through the bottom of a mud puddle, like they expected, they twirled through a whirlpool of water and were propelled high into the air on a geyser.

"I think the forest sprang a leak!" Shelby shouted. The geyser lost its energy, and they splashed down into the water.

When they swam to the surface and popped their heads out of the water, they were met by a sight that could only be described as enchanting.

"Wow, it does exist!" Shelby said as she wiped the water from her eyes. Just a short distance away, rising up into rainbow-colored clouds, was the magnificent Walla Wunga Castle made of diamonds and pearls.

Ricky and Shelby doggy-paddled their way to shore and stepped out onto a beach of sparkling white sand. Their fur coats instantly dried under the warm sunshine.

Shelby was in awe as she looked all around . . . from the unicorns passing through the clouds, to the mist that sprayed from the gold and silver waterfall, to the overwhelming sense of peace she felt as she listened to the soothing sounds of the songbirds. "It is more beautiful than I could have ever imagined," she said.

Ricky was just as amazed. "This is truly a land of wonder," he thought.

A purple and blue butterfly landed on the tip of Shelby's nose. For the first time in a long time, they were able to relax and laugh. The butterfly smiled, flapped its wings, and flew gently away.

"Welcome," said a voice. Shelby and Ricky looked back toward the castle. A streak of light whirled through the palm trees and twirled around the waterfall. Silver and blue stars trickled down upon Ricky and Shelby.

Out of the light appeared Nia, the Woodland Spirit. "Welcome to my humble home," she said as she floated through the mist on white fluorescent wings.

Shelby and Ricky were just as mesmerized by her beauty as the orphaned animals were. She was dressed in a short, wavy green gown and her long, silky brown hair was adorned with roses and white lilies.

"We must be lost in a dream," Ricky said. It was the only way to explain it.

The Woodland Spirit landed on the waterfall. She lifted her wings, and a million ladybugs filled the sky.

"It isn't a dream, my dear child," Nia said to Ricky. "I'm simply here to thank you."

"Thank us?" Ricky said. "We're the ones who should be thanking you, for helping us out of the swamp."

"No, Ricky," she replied. "I merely cleared a path. The love you have for each other, your family and friends, and Walla Wunga Forest has brought you here this day. That love has instilled in both of you courage that is far more powerful than me. So today I thank you, Shelby and Ricky, for your courage. It has overwhelmed my heart with joy. You have faced many obstacles, and although you may not realize it, your will is stronger than ever. No matter what happens from this point forward, always be proud of who you are."

Shelby bowed her head and started to cry. Nia didn't have to ask why. She could read it in her tears. Though her words were comforting, they were only words. "I know you are both tired and scared, and every path seems bumpier than the last."

"You can say that again," Ricky replied. "You couldn't, by chance, just spin your magic wand and make it all go away?"

Nia smiled. "I'm sorry, Ricky, I wish I could. I can clear a path, but I cannot interfere with Mother Nature. Mother can be quite brilliant, as you can see when you look around, but, just between you and me, she can also be quite moody at times, especially if one tries to outwit her. There is an old saying: Fool with Mother Nature and you become the fool."

She twirled her finger, and an image appeared in the water rushing down the fall. It was that of Harley the Hunter being chased by the swarm of bees. “And speaking of such a fool,” Nia said.

Shelby’s brother then appeared in the waves. “David,” Shelby mumbled under her breath. At that moment, all the terrible memories of leaving her brother behind flashed before her eyes.

Nia lifted off the waterfall and floated over to Shelby. She knew all about her family’s encounter with Harley. “I know you worry about your brother David,” Nia said.

“Yes, very much. It is so hard not knowing whether he’s okay,” she replied with a sniffle.

“Worry no more, my dear child,” Nia replied. “I cannot bring your brother home, but I can tell you he is okay, and is surrounded by animals who love him very much. I can also tell you that he thinks of you and the rest of his family every day and every night. And he knows, in his heart, you are thinking of him.”

“Really?” Shelby said. “He is okay?” “Yes, Shelby. In fact, I hear he takes after his big sister when it comes to pitching. They say he can toss an acorn wicked fast.”

The three of them had a good laugh. “And speaking of pitching, that was quite a display you two put on against Dredd. Even Mother Nature got a kick out of that one. Oh, and Ricky, just a tip from Mother Nature: Keep that elbow up when you follow through with your swing. You were dipping a bit.”

“I will, Nia. I will,” Ricky chuckled.

“One thing,” Shelby said, “before we go. Can you tell us if Tombstone still has the cell phone?” Nia grinned.

“I’m sorry, Shelby. There is a purpose to everything in life. For reasons you will soon come to understand, I cannot reveal the answer to that mystery.”

Nia flapped her wings and rose above the waterfall. There was still doubt in Ricky and Shelby's eyes, but there was also renewed hope.

"Your journey continues. There is still more to be done. I wish I could say it will be easy, but I cannot. But always remember and never forget the words of your friend Merlin: Believe in the magic and you shall overcome."

Nia flicked her finger, and Ricky and Shelby disappeared.

CHAPTER 14
Mouse Trap

With Harley no longer a threat, Kristen quickly pranced over to the Ranger Station and peeked through a window. Ranger Mike's deputy, Norm, was the only one inside. His walkie-talkie was on the table in front of him. The only problem: He was laying back in his chair, snoring up a storm.

"What am I going to do?" She wondered. "I certainly can't knock on the door and hand him the note." She bowed her head and noticed a tiny opening near the bottom of the wall. She squatted down and peeked inside.

"Hello, anyone home?" She asked.

"Who wants to know?" A squeaky voice snapped back.

"My name is Kristen. I'm a white-tailed deer," she replied. A tiny head popped out of the hole.

"Oh, hello there," said a mouse. "Sorry, but you can never be too safe around here. Knucklehead Norm is always setting traps. But anyway, welcome to my home. My name is Celo. What can I do for you, Kristen?"

"I need you to wake up the deputy and give him this note. I

can slide it under the front door. Ranger Mike is in trouble, and he needs help – and fast," she said.

"WHAT! Save a ranger?" Shouted Celo, "Are you crazy, lady? He is the enemy! Never a day goes by that Norm and the other deputies don't try to capture our hides! Oh sure, they use those humane traps so we do not get hurt. Well, whoop-de-doo, aren't we lucky. While they relax in cozy comfort, we are outside roasting in the summer and freezing our cabooses off in the winter. Even if you built me my own personal cheese factory, I wouldn't help. No way, not a chance, isn't happening, forget about it!"

"Please, if not for Ranger Mike, then do it for me," she begged.

Celo let out a sigh as he watched a sad tear trickle from Kristen's eye. "Oh no. Don't start blubbering," he said. "All right, all right, I'll help... just please, turn the faucet off."

"Thank you, Celo. Thank you from the bottom of my heart." And she leaned down and gave him a kiss.

"Yuck! Yuck! And triple yuck!" He said as he tried to wipe the kiss away.

Kristen walked up the handicap ramp, placed the note on the welcome mat, and shuffled it under the front door with her right front hoof.

Celo gathered his four brothers, Cisco, Chico, Carlo, and Ralph. "We have a dangerous mission," he said. He went on to explain what needed to be done. They were not too keen on the idea, but agreed to help for Kristen's sake.

"We'll have to do this ninja style," Celo said.

The brothers covered their fur in black soot and made their way through a series of secret passageways under the Ranger Station.

"Alright, guys," Celo said. "No mistakes or they'll be dragging us out to the garbage by the tail."

They climbed up the wiring in the wall on the far end of the station. Celo stopped halfway and walked into the hollowed-out head of a bear mounted on the wall. He peeked through the bear's eyes and glanced around the room, making sure the coast was clear.

He signaled to his brothers, and they continued climbing the wiring toward the ceiling. Once at the ceiling, Carlo popped out a tiny piece of tile in the corner near the wall. One by one they squeezed through the hole and dropped onto the coat rack below. Using the coats as camouflage, they slid down the metal pole and dropped to the floor.

Celo turned. "Ralph, keep an eye on the rear."

"Will do, bro," he replied.

The five of them zigzagged their way over to the door, retrieved the note, and cautiously made their way to the table where Norm was snoozing.

Cisco, Chico, Carlo, and Ralph hopped on each other's shoulders to form a ladder. Celo then crawled up their backs and latched onto the tablecloth. He slowly climbed his way up, suddenly stopping a few inches from the top. The faint smell of cheddar cheese and peanut butter was in the air.

Sniff! Sniff! "As I suspected," said Celo as he peeked over the edge. The table was loaded with mousetraps. But these were not humane traps. They were Snapper 2000 mousetraps, the most diabolical in the business. They were shaped like giant chunks of Swiss cheese with peanut butter in the center. The mouse would stick his or her head inside and BAM! The trap would snap and adios, amigo.

The deadly traps didn't really concern Celo. He was always

outwitting Norm. In fact, there was a far greater chance of Norm being whacked by one of his own traps than a member of Celo's family getting caught.

Celo tiptoed across the table, made a string out of paper clips, and lowered it down to the ground. His brothers hooked the note to the string, and Celo pulled it up. He dragged the note across the table, making sure to steer clear of the traps, and placed it near the bowl of soup Norm was having for lunch.

Celo took a look inside the bowl. "Pea soup, yuck!" He said. He then stood on his hind legs and let out an ear-piercing whistle. Norm's nose twitched, and he mumbled under his breath, but he didn't wake up.

"Okay, you asked for it: Slam Dunk!" Celo said. He scooted up Norm's shoulder and tried to push his head forward so his face would fall into the soup. "Come on, cement-head," but he couldn't get it to budge. He collapsed to his hind knees out of breath.

Celo realized there was only one option left: the Super Soaker. Climb to the top of Norm's head, jump, and land on the front edge of the soup bowl in the hope that the back end of the bowl lifts up and super soaks his face with every last bit of mushy green mess.

Celo climbed what was left of Norm's hair and stepped onto his bald spot. He thought about leaving a little "surprise" behind, but the look Kristen gave him through the window squashed the idea. "Just kidding," he said.

He stepped to the edge of Norm's brow and looked down. "Rats," he said. There was a big problem, and it was Norm's nose. It was huge. "Look at the size of that honker," he said. "Man. I would hate to be his handkerchief," and whistled down to his brother Cisco for help.

Cisco quickly joined his brother on Norm's head. "I need a little boost to clear Norm's schnozzola," he said.

"I gotcha, Celo. Let's do it on a count of three." Cisco grabbed his brother at the waist. "Ready?' Cisco asked. "As I'll ever be," Celo replied.

"One, two, three!"

Cisco launched Celo into the air and let go. "Yikes!" Celo shouted. Norm exhaled, and a booger dangling from one of his nose hairs swung out and gave Celo a whack. Luckily, Celo was able to steady himself just in time to nail the landing.

The far end of the bowl lifted up as planned, and the green mushy mess splashed out and SPLAT! Norm got soaked.

He leaped out of his seat, hitting the table with his knee on the way up. "Look out below!" Celo shouted as the mousetraps flew everywhere. Suddenly Norm's eyes bulged wide, and a wicked pain rose up his spine and rang his brain.

"OUCH!" He shouted. One of his mousetraps slammed shut on his right big toe. He danced around on one foot and "OUCH!" He screamed again. Another trap slammed shut on his left big toe.

Norm quickly removed the mousetraps and flung them against the wall. His two big toes were beet red, throbbing with pain, and had swelled to the size of light bulbs.

Norm waddled like a duck out the door and opened up an ice chest that contained bottles of water for the rangers. He frantically tossed out the bottles and quickly buried his feet into the ice. "My toesies," he said, "my poor little toesies."

Kristen poked open the window with her nose. "What now?" She asked Celo. It was obvious; Norm would be of no use to them.

Celo shook his head and shrugged his shoulders. Just then, static screeched from Norm's walkie-talkie.

"Hmmm," Celo said. "It might be a long shot, but maybe, just maybe it will work."

"What will work?" Kristen asked.

"Just watch," Celo said. He hopped onto the walkie-talkie, cleared his throat, pressed down on the talk button, and did his best impression of Norm. "Mayday! Mayday!" He said in a deep, raspy voice. "Ranger Mike's airplane crash-landed near the Mighty Moses. I need a search and rescue helicopter on the double."

He hopped off the button and waited for a response. Five seconds turned to ten, ten seconds turned to twenty. Celo, Cisco, Chico, Carlo, Ralph, and Kristen closed their eyes and prayed for the silence to be broken.

And their prayer was answered. "That's a 10-4, Norm. This is Ranger Shaun. I'm at the heliport. The weather is very poor on Mount Chubaluba, but I'm on my way."

"Yeah!" They shouted. Celo stepped back on the talk button. "10-4, Shaun. Bring him home safely."

"You can count on it," he replied. "Over and out."

Kristen turned to Celo and his brothers. "Thank you," she said, all misty-eyed. They smiled back.

Celo stepped to the edge of the table and looked down, "What a day!" He said. They were able to help Kristen, Norm got whacked, and most delicious of all: The floor was covered with pieces of cheese and slabs of peanut butter from the broken traps. "Oh, baby! We're going to eat well tonight," he said.

Kristen backed away from the window. "Hmm," she said. "I need to let the others know help is on the way, but how?"

"I'll take care of that for you," said a bald eagle named Lincoln from his cage. The rangers had set up a bird sanctuary to treat and then release injured birds.

Lincoln plucked a feather from his tail and picked the lock.

"Where did you learn to do that?" She asked.

"This? It's no big deal. I do it all the time."

"Are you sure your wing is strong enough to fly?"

"For Ranger Mike, I'm willing to take the chance," he replied.

Lincoln had hurt his right wing during a blizzard last winter. He couldn't see very well due to the driving snow and slammed his wing into a tree branch.

"Ranger Mike traipsed through a foot and a half of snow in the freezing cold to help me last winter," Lincoln said as he pushed open the cage and spread out his massive seven-foot wings. "I will complete this mission or die trying."

"Thank you for your service," Kristen replied. Lincoln gave her a salute and took to the sky.

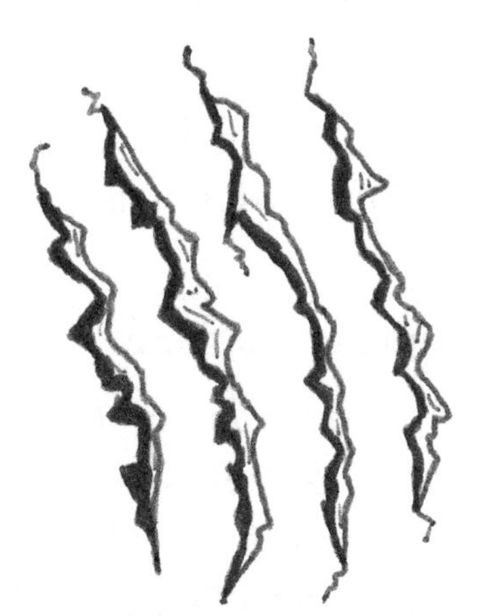

CHAPTER 15
Tombstone's Lair

Shelby and Ricky opened their eyes and found themselves at the foot of Tombstone's lair.

They huddled closely together and entered. The lair was dark and damp, and the sound of dripping water made each step more nerve-wracking than the last.

If they were going to find Ranger Mike's phone and slip away without a trace, they would have to be quick and just as quiet.

"Ricky! Over there!" Shelby whispered. A streak of light cracked through the rock ceiling and beamed down on Ranger Mike's cell phone sitting in an old tree stump. Shelby moved toward the phone.

"This is too easy," Ricky thought. "Wait," he said, and stopped her with his paw.

Ricky's instinct was right on the nose, but unfortunately a little tardy. Tombstone snuck up behind them with his claws drawn. "Looking for something?" He asked. Shelby and Ricky slowly turned around.

Tombstone could not believe it. "You two again? You just

don't know when to quit, I see. Well, maybe I can put an end to it for you."

Tombstone lifted up on his hind legs and let out a ferocious roar. Shelby and Ricky ducked down as low as they could go to protect themselves.

"What on earth is going on out here?"

Ricky and Shelby turned. Out of the shadows of the lair appeared another mountain lion. It was obvious by her voice the lion was a female. She stepped forward with a rather angry look on her face, but it wasn't aimed at Ricky or Shelby.

She looked right past them. "Theodore? Was that you making the awful noise?"

Shelby and Ricky looked at each other. "Theodore?" They said.

"Yes," the female lion replied. "Theodore is my son. My name is Stella."

"Oh. My name is Ricky and this is my friend Shelby," Ricky said.

Stella smiled. "It is very nice to meet you two. What brings you to my lair?"

"They are my friends," Tombstone interrupted. He knew he had to come up with an excuse and fast. He didn't want his mom to know the truth. "I was just . . . um . . . I was just giving my friends here a dancing lesson."

"A dancing lesson?" Stella replied. She knew Theodore was telling a fib. Every time he did, his upper lip would quiver. "Is this true, Ricky?" She asked.

"Well, not exactly," Ricky said.

"Yeah," Shelby added. "It was more like a cooking lesson,

and we were the main course. Your son was just about to eat us."

"Eat you? That is not possible. We are vegetarians. We do not eat meat."

"Seriously?" Shelby replied. She could not believe what she was hearing. She had just learned Tombstone's real name was Theodore, and now this? A vegetarian mountain lion? That was about as absurd as saying Harley the Hunter was a good person, just misunderstood.

"He was also threatening to eat our friends and Ranger Mike," Ricky said.

"Ranger Mike?" She said. Her face went from angry to steaming hot mad. "Theodore Octavius Lion III! What were you thinking? Do you know who Ranger Mike is?"

"Um . . . no," he replied with a pout.

"Let me refresh your memory." She turned to Shelby and Ricky and explained how her family came to know Ranger Mike.

"Theodore was always a curious cub. When he was three months old he wandered too close to the edge of the lair. A stone broke free, and Theodore fell to a ledge below. I was terrified. There is nothing worse than seeing your cub in trouble and not being able to help."

"I'm sure," Shelby replied. "It must have been awful."

"Later that day a ranger's airplane passed overhead. The next thing I knew, a ranger scaled down the mountain on a rope. He scooped Theodore up and brought him back home. Besides giving birth to Theodore, it was the happiest moment of my life."

Stella then turned to her son. "Do you know who that ranger was, Theodore?" She asked.

He bowed his head with embarrassment as the memories of that day came back to him. "Ranger Mike?" He asked.

"Yes. He risked his life to save yours, and you pay him back by threatening to eat him? Why, Theodore? What has gotten into you?"

Tombstone's bottom lip popped out. "I wasn't really trying to eat them, just trying to scare them."

"Why on earth would you do that?"

"'Cause that's what mountain lions do. We are the rulers of the forest."

"My gosh, you have been listening to stories from your grandfather again, haven't you?"

"Yes, Mom. But that isn't the only reason. It was also because of him," he said, pointing to Ricky.

"Me?" Ricky replied.

"I was walking by your house one day and overheard you reading from a book. You said a mountain lion was the ruler of the forest, with a heart filled with bravery, feared by all creatures big and small.

"Then, while walking home, I came upon a family of woodchucks. They stopped in front of me. I said, 'I'm the ruler of this forest,' and ROARED! They looked at each other and started laughing at me.

"A little further down the path a group of humans saw me. You should have seen the look on their faces; they were terrified. I took a step forward, and they jammed into their jeep and took off, leaving all their camping gear behind. It made me feel good."

"How many times have I told you not to worry about what other animals think?"

"I know, Mom. I know."

"A lion doesn't scare with threats. A bully does that. And yes, Theodore, the heart of a lion is filled with bravery, but that bravery is not a given right; it has to be earned."

Stella turned her attention to Ricky and Shelby. "I want to apologize to the both of you for my son's actions. Is there anything I can do to make it up to you?"

"The phone," Ricky said. "Behind you. It belongs to Ranger Mike." Ricky went on to explain the accident and how Theodore stole the phone from the Weasel Brothers. "It might be our only chance to get help for Ranger Mike."

Stella picked up the phone and dangled it in front of Ricky and Shelby. It was a mangled mess. "Sorry," Theodore replied. "I stumbled and dropped the phone on a rock."

Ricky and Shelby were devastated. "Thanks anyway," Ricky said. "We'd better be getting back."

Ricky and Shelby left the lair with their lives intact, but they were no closer to saving Ranger Mike. And that made them very sad. But they knew, as they stepped out of the lair and into the stinging wind and rain, they had to put aside their disappointment. There was no time to feel sorry for themselves or be angry. It would take all their concentration to make it down the long, winding dirt road to the valley below. One mistake could cost them dearly. Tombstone may have no longer posed a threat, but the Wind Dragon was more dangerous than ever.

CHAPTER 16
A Flicker of Hope

The animals of Walla Wunga Forest huddled in their homes, trying their best to block out the sounds of the Wind Dragon by covering their ears. What they couldn't do, however, was silence their fears. What would become of their forest? Every wicked thought imaginable entered into their minds.

Would it be turned into another Samp Mortar Swamp with insects one hundred times their normal size? Or maybe the forest would be set ablaze for all eternity and ruled by giant fire-breathing serpents.

Whichever it turned out to be, one thing was for certain in their minds: Walla Wunga Forest would never be the same again.

However, even in the darkest of times a ray of light can shine. Lincoln the Bald Eagle soared across the sky, spreading the good news to all the animals of Walla Wunga Forest.

"Operation Friendship! Help is on the way!" He yelled to Big Stanley as he zoomed by on the dune buggy. "GREEEEATTTTTT NEWWWWWWSSSSSSS!"

Next up, he flew over the farmhouse: "Operation Friendship is a success!" He yelled to Lauren.

"Wonderful news, darling!" She yelled back with a perky smile, and gave Lincoln a wave with her freshly manicured paw. Lincoln passed over the edge of the cliff and glided effortlessly across. "Operation Friendship. Help is on the way."

Jasper, Annie, and the gang saluted Lincoln as he flew by. They were elated to hear the good news.

Running Wolf was retracing his steps back to his pack when Lincoln flew by. "Operation Friendship. Help is on the way."

Running Wolf stopped and looked up into the pelting rain. "Spirit, you have guided me well," he said. "Please bless Lincoln's wings with the same fortune."

Lincoln sailed down the side of Mount Lulu. Earl the Mountain Goat was taking cover under an evergreen tree that was swaying in the wind. Lincoln settled on a large branch and wiped the rain from his eyes with the back of his wing.

Earl and Lincoln had been neighbors growing up. Earl and his family lived in a shallow cave under an old redwood tree growing out of the mountain. Lincoln and his family lived in the pine tree.

"Good news, old friend," he said. "Help is on the way for Ranger Mike. I'm trying to make my way back to Mighty Moses to let everyone know, but the strength of the Wind Dragon is posing a mighty challenge."

"Follow the riverbank. It is your best bet, Lincoln," Earl advised. "It might take you a bit longer, but it will be safer."

"Yeah," Lincoln replied. "Good idea."

"Just remember to stay low. If you fly too high and the wind gets hold of your wings, you'll nosedive into the river. That will be the end of the line. Louie the Pike will make sure of that."

"Thanks for the advice, my friend. I'd better get going."

"The best of luck to you. Safe travels."

"I'll see you soon, my friend," Lincoln said.

Lincoln took Earl's advice and stayed as close to the raging Walla Wunga River as he could. As he approached the bottom of Razor's Edge Falls, he noticed Bodhi trying his best to battle his way up the river, but the storm was just too powerful. One hop forward, four hops back. "Need a ride, my little green buddy?" He asked as he met up with him.

"Groovy, bald dude! Windsurfing eagle style," he replied and hopped onto Lincoln's back. "Let's rock!"

Lincoln tried to lift off, but he couldn't, not because of Bodhi's extra weight, but because of the wind that was blowing down from the top of Razor's Edge Falls. It was incredible. Lincoln knew that even with the strength of his seven-foot wings, there was a good chance that if he tried scaling the falls, the Wind Dragon's fury would force him into the raging water and thus into the jaws of Louie the Pike and his gang.

"I think it's time to call in for backup," he said, and let out a series of squawks and clicking sounds.

Within seconds, out of the wind and rain appeared a flock of his old eagle buddies. Though they had not flown together for years, they would come to each other's aid at a moment's notice. Five of the eagles landed to his left and five to his right, forming a wing the width of a jumbo jet – and just as powerful.

"Welcome, boys," Lincoln said. "Follow me!"

"American pride!" They shouted together and flapped their mighty wings. The eleven bald eagles, to the dismay of Louie and his gang, swiftly scaled the falls and headed for the Mighty Moses.

CHAPTER 17
Final Stand

Ricky and Shelby were struggling down the mountainside. "This is going to take forever," Shelby shouted through the wind and rain. Ricky paused a moment. It was raining so hard, the water was flowing down the mountain like a river.

Ricky looked at Shelby. "Are you thinking what I'm thinking?" He asked.

Shelby smiled back. "You betcha," she replied.

Ricky peeled away a large piece of bark from a dead tree and placed it in the river. "Hop on, Shelby," he said, and they rode the muddy river to the valley below.

They met Bart and Barry, the Beaver Brothers, and Satch the Copperhead Snake by the Mighty Moses. The wind was blowing so strong they could barely keep their paws on the ground. Even Satch was having a hard time keeping from rolling over.

Bart could tell by the looks on their faces that Shelby and Ricky didn't have good news. Ricky shook his head. "No luck," he said.

A howling wind whirled through the Mighty Moses. The word 'REVENGE' could be heard in its wake. They slowly turned around toward the oak tree.

A lightning bolt flashed from the sky, splitting the Mighty Moses right down the middle of its trunk. The two pieces of the tree fell off to the sides like a stage curtain opening.

Through the darkness appeared a massive funnel of wind. From its evil red eye to its fangs of fire, lightning wings, and rotting bones, the Wind Dragon was more sinister than they could have ever imagined. "That is one nasty sucker!" Barry said.

"As nasty as they come," Bart agreed.

Out of the depths of the Wind Dragon's fury was spawned a second, third, fourth, and fifth Wind Dragon. Within seconds, the Wind Dragon's army was fifty funnels strong. It had vowed to destroy everything in its path. That path was now as long as the forest was wide.

The Wind Dragon flapped its wings and launched a lightning bolt toward the peak of Mount Chubaluba. The lightning bolt exploded, creating a massive rockslide. It was the animals' double worst nightmare: a forest buried in stone. With no food to eat or water to drink, every single animal, tree, flower, twig, and blade of grass in Walla Wunga Forest would become extinct.

The Wind Dragon roared, flames drooling from its mouth, and it began twisting toward the five friends, tossing trees aside as if they were mere pencils.

Regardless of the danger, Ricky and the others had only one thing on their mind: Ranger Mike's safety.

"What do we do? We are running out of time!" Shelby said.

The piece of parachute covering the hole blew away. "Go! Don't worry about me!" Ranger Mike replied with a grimace as he sat up in the hole. Mike could tell by the ferocity of the wind and rain that a dangerous storm was approaching.

“I will never forget what you did for me today, but it is time to go home to your families! I don’t know what is going to become of us, but one thing I do know is that I will forever be grateful to all of you. Now please, for me, go home!”

The five of them stepped back from the hole. They did not tell Ranger Mike about the Wind Dragons. It wouldn’t have done any good if they did. Only the animals could see the dragons. Nor did they mention the fact that their fate was already sealed. There was no way they could survive the wrath of the Wind Dragons or the rockslide, but Ranger Mike could.

They looked up into the blackened sky one last time, hoping against hope for that one ray of light to shine through. “If help hasn’t arrived by now, I’m afraid it never will,“ Bart said sadly.

Shelby began to cry. “It’s okay,” Ricky said, and he hugged her tight.

“Hey, wait a minute, do you hear that?“ Satch asked.

“Hear what?“ Bart replied.

“Listen,“ Satch said, and they all lifted their ears.

Lincoln and his team appeared through the wind-blown trees. Bodhi was standing on his wing, waving his hand in the air. “Operation Friendship, baby!” Bodhi shouted. Lincoln navigated his way through the wind and landed on a tree stump near the hole. “A helicopter is on the way!” Bodhi said, and he did a double flip to the ground.

Barry and his brother were ecstatic. "Yes!" Barry shouted, and he and Bart leaped into the rain and gave each other a stinging high paw.

Ricky was not nearly as encouraged. "What good will a helicopter do?" He said. He was right. "There is nowhere for the helicopter to land. There are too many trees."

Ricky knew there was only one option left. They needed to lift Ranger Mike out of the hole and carry him to the open field across the stream. "This way the helicopter would be able to lower a rescue bucket, and Ranger Mike could crawl inside and be lifted to safety," Ricky said.

"It just isn't possible," Satch replied. "The seven of us are not strong enough to lift Ranger Mike out of the hole. And even if by some miracle we could, there is no way we would be able to outrun the Wind Dragon and its army."

Or could they?

"Yes we can," spoke a voice. "Let me help."

Bart, Barry, and Satch slowly turned around to find Tombstone standing before them. From one nightmare to another, they thought.

Even though the Wind Dragon's power was deafening, at that moment a quiet calm fell over the forest, almost as if things were happening in slow motion. Shelby stepped toward Tombstone.

"No! Not again!" Barry shouted, and reached out to stop her.

Ricky lifted his paw. "It is okay, Barry. Trust me," he said to him.

Shelby burst out with a smile. "Yes," she said. "You can help, Theodore. Thank you!" Shelby knew if anyone could lift Ranger Mike out of the hole, it was Theodore.

Ricky glanced up into the raindrops, and the words uttered by Nia the Woodland Spirit whispered through his ears: "There is a purpose to everything in life. For reasons you will soon come to understand, I cannot reveal the answer to that mystery."

It was now clear to Ricky what Nia had meant. If she had told them about the phone being broken, they would have never ventured into Tombstone's lair. Tombstone would have remained their enemy instead of becoming a friend.

Bart, Barry, and Satch were quite bewildered. They had the same looks on their faces as Ranger Mike did when he learned the animals could talk. In fact, all the animals hiding in their homes dropped their paws from their ears and poked their heads outside. "Theodore?" Everyone asked.

"There is no time to explain," Ricky said. He glanced back over his shoulder. The Wind Dragon and its army were bearing down upon them, the rockslide not far behind.

"We only have seconds," Ricky said. "Theodore? Do you think you can climb into the hole and lift Ranger Mike out?"

"You bet I can!" Theodore said. "Just watch me." Without a moment of hesitation, he leaped into the hole, dug his head under Ranger Mike's body, and rolled him onto his back.

Ranger Mike grimaced again. "Thank you, Theodore," Mike said and patted him on the head. Theodore stood there motionless; he was amazed that Ranger Mike had remembered him. "Your mom would be very proud."

A feeling of peace came over Theodore's body. He now knew what his mom meant about bravery having to be earned. He also realized that bravery was not about strength or fear, but rather love and the willingness to fight for what you believe in.

"You saved my life, Ranger Mike. It's time for me to repay the favor. Now let's get you home."

Theodore pushed off with his powerful hind legs and launched out of the hole.

"Hurry!" Shelby yelled out. The Wind Dragons were closing in.

Lincoln and his flock flew out in front of Theodore to cut down some of the wind, and Ricky, Shelby, Bart, and Barry helped by pushing from behind.

The Wind Dragon and its army roared past Mount Chubaluba. "Hurry, hurry!" Shelby screamed through the wind. "We need to go faster!"

Theodore dug down deep. "No quitting!" He grunted through his clenched teeth, and picked up the pace.

They crossed over the stream and made it to the open field just as the helicopter twirled out of the clouds.

Theodore gently laid Ranger Mike onto the ground.

The animals backed away and took cover in the tall grass. Ranger Mike frantically waved his arms over his head to try and get the attention of Shaun, the helicopter pilot, and it worked. Shaun turned around and positioned the helicopter right above him. The helicopter door opened up, and the rescue bucket began lowering.

For Shelby and Ricky, this was the most nerve-wracking part of the whole ordeal. Every second seemed like an eternity; they were so close to saving Ranger Mike.

"Please, please, please," Shelby said as she closed her eyes. She couldn't bear to watch.

Ranger Mike looked over his shoulder. The tornadoes were bearing down on him. He reached out and grabbed the bottom of the bucket as it swayed his way. He quickly unlocked the door latch and crawled inside. He shut the door and gave Shaun the thumbs-up sign.

As the rescue bucket started to rise, Shaun, to be on the

safe side, began maneuvering the helicopter away from the approaching tornadoes.

"We did it!" Ricky said. Shelby opened her eyes. She had never been so happy in all her life. "Operation Friendship! Mission accomplished!"

The Wind Dragon and its army crossed over the stream. It would only be a matter of seconds before Ricky, Shelby, and their friends met their fate.

"We made the right choice," Ricky said as he watched the helicopter disappear over the treetops.

"Yes we did, Ricky," Shelby replied. "Ranger Mike would have done the same for us."

"You guys make a run for it. I have your backs," Theodore said, rising up on his hind legs and facing the Wind Dragon head on.

Ricky, however, had had enough. "No, Theodore. I'm done running," Ricky said. "Me too," Shelby agreed. So did Bart, Barry, and Satch.

Shelby and Ricky looked at each other for what they figured to be the last time. Ricky held out his paw, and Shelby grabbed it tightly. "You're the best friend anyone could ever ask for!" Ricky said. "You'll forever be in my heart," Shelby replied and gave him a peck on the cheek.

Shelby, Ricky, and their friends stepped alongside Theodore with their heads held high.

The Wind Dragon roared to a stop a few feet away, and its winds calmed. "I shall give you a fighting chance," a voice grumbled from the depths of the dragon. "You have ten seconds to run."

"No! This is our home!" Ricky shouted. "We are done running. Ranger Mike is safe, and that is all that matters to us. We accept our fate."

"Is he now?" The Wind Dragon said. "Never underestimate my power."

The Wind Dragon lifted its wings, and two dragon vultures, the size of pterodactyls, flew out of the pit of its belly. The Wind Dragon let out a diabolical laugh. "Bring the helicopter down!" He ordered. "And afterwards, you can feed on the carcasses."

The dragon vultures did not hesitate. They spit fire from their mouths and headed out on their mission.

"We are sorry for calling you a Bubbles. It was wrong of us to do so. We meant no harm. Please, please don't do this," Shelby pleaded. "Find it in your heart to let Ranger Mike go."

The Wind Dragon roared with laughter. "The only heart you will find within these rotting bones is a black heart, filled with evil and destruction. And if you think, for even a second, this has been about a lousy nickname, you're even more foolish than I thought. Your request for a peaceful end is denied!"

Then something totally unexpected happened. The forest opened up, and all the animals crawled from their homes. Not to make a run for it, but to join Ricky, Shelby, and their friends.

The animals formed a line of defense as far as the eye could see. Ricky stepped forward. "We will fight as one to the very end. In the name of Operation Friendship," he said.

The animals' solidarity did little to impress the Wind Dragon. "And so it shall be," the Dragon replied with an arrogant laugh. "My revenge shall be all the sweeter!"

The Wind Dragon raised his wings to strike, and he ordered his army to do the same.

"Wait just one minute."

The Wind Dragon paused and shifted its eye to Merlin, who had landed on a tree branch.

"These animals have caused you no harm. Leave them be and call off the dragon vultures. Blow away now and all will be forgotten. Enough is enough already!"

The Wind Dragon calmed. Did he see the light? Would he follow Merlin's advice? The animals wondered. "Not a chance," Bart said, and he was right.

"Foolish old owl! Your words of wisdom are laughable," the Wind Dragon said and flicked his wing. A gust of wind blew Merlin over, and he landed upside-down against the tree's trunk. "Now it's time to end this!" The Wind Dragon said.

Once again he lifted his wings. His army followed suit.

"Ricky!" Shelby whispered. "Look!"

A whirling tail of light appeared, seemingly out of nowhere, and beautiful music filled the air. The light gently whirled itself around the Wind Dragon, to his displeasure.

"What is this annoyance?" The Wind Dragon said as he unsuccessfully tried to swat the light away with his wing.

A hush fell over the animals as the light twirled before the Wind Dragon's eye. It brightened and exploded, raining silver and blue stars down upon the forest. Out of the light appeared Nia the Woodland Spirit.

"Hello, Ricky and Shelby. Thank you for everything you two have done. Thanks to all of you. Your courage here today has filled my heart with great joy." She then spun around and looked straight into the eye of the Wind Dragon. "I'll take it from here," she said.

"I was hoping you would show," the Wind Dragon said as they both stared each other down. "I couldn't care less about name-calling or these little rodent friends of yours. This is the moment

I have been waiting a thousand years for! I seek my revenge on you, Woodland Spirit! You may have defeated me twice in the past, but I am back, more powerful than ever, with an army of devastation and a million boulders strong! It will give me great pleasure to watch you suffer."

"I promised the animals of Walla Wunga Forest I'd protect them," Nia replied. "All I asked in return was for the animals to treat each other with love and kindness. Words you obviously do not know the meaning of. And, as you can tell by looking behind me, they have done their part. It is time I do mine."

The Wind Dragon showed Nia no respect. It simply laughed. "Your attempt to stop me will be futile. My army and I will not be denied!"

"Well, maybe not you, but I think your army has had a change of heart," Merlin said as he flipped over.

The Wind Dragon slowly turned around. "Gulp!"

His army was retreating. In doing so, they were blowing the massive boulders back up the mountain.

"What's the meaning of this?" The Wind Dragon demanded.

"Sorry, dude, we didn't sign up for this," said one of the retreating dragons. "You're on your own."

The dragons knew better than to tangle with Nia on her home turf. She may have come across as a gentle soul, but if you crossed her, especially at the expense of the forest, watch out. Much like Mother Nature, she could deliver a serious wallop.

The Wind Dragon swung its head back. "Who needs them? I shall take care of you myself!" He said defiantly. "You stopped me from burning the forest to the ground a thousand years ago and from turning this wretched place into swampland a hundred years ago, but today, Woodland Spirit, your reign ends. For I made a promise as well. To silence this forest FOREVER MORE!"

He laughed. "I have a few words of wisdom myself: Three times is the charm."

The Wind Dragon lifted his wings a final time and let his fury loose just as Nia snapped her fingers.

"Take cover!" The animals shouted, and they buried their heads in the ground. A massive explosion rocked the forest – an explosion so powerful it lit up the forest with the energy of a million suns.

When the dust settled, Ricky was shocked to find he was still breathing. "This is freaky weird," Ricky said as he poked his head up. He looked over to Shelby, and she was also alive. In fact, all the animals survived. Not only that, but the rain and wind had stopped as well.

"Victory is mine!" The Wind Dragon shouted triumphantly. The animals slowly looked up. The Wind Dragon's voice was no longer deep and wicked. It was rather soft and squeaky, like a mouse's voice.

The Wind Dragon noticed it as well. He coughed to clear his throat. "I mean, victory is mine!" He shouted again. His voice didn't change. It was then that he realized what was happening.

"Oh no! Oh no! What have you done to me, Woodland Spirit?" He said as he looked at himself. "You turned me into a soft summer breeze."

"The third time is a charm? That is a good one," Nia replied, sitting alongside Merlin on the tree branch, no worse for wear. "But I think a much more fitting line for this occasion would be..." She paused in mid-thought and looked over at Shelby. "Would you like to take this one, dear?"

"With pleasure," Shelby replied.

Shelby dusted off her fur and looked into the shrunken eye of the Wind Dragon.

"Three strikes and you're out!" She said, and all the animals roared.

"That is what you think. I'll be back. Just you wait and see!" The Wind Dragon replied, and blew harmlessly away.

The dark, menacing clouds faded along with the Wind Dragon, and were replaced by blue skies and sunshine. The warm air returned, as did all the birds. Even the eerie mist over Samp Mortar Swamp lifted, and the insects shrunk back to their normal size.

Ricky brushed the mud and weeds from his fur. "We did it!" He said to himself. Finally, it was over.

"Not so fast," Bart said, pointing to the sky. All the animals gathered in horror. "Ranger Mike! The dragon vultures! They're moving in for the kill."

But this day would not end on such a sorrowful note. A silhouette appearedin the skies above the helicopter. The silhouette vaguely resembled that of a woman's face.

Shelby quickly turned to Nia. "Mother Nature?" She whispered. Nia didn't say a word. She simply replied with a smile.

A drop of light fell from the silhouette and twirled through the helicopter's propeller, forming a magnificent spinning prism. The light flashed across the sky as far as the eye could see.

The dragon vultures flew out from under the helicopter and into the light. The massive creatures were transformed into a pair of harmless gnats. They flew head on into the helicopter and SPLAT! They became windshield meat. Ranger Shaun then swiped the mess away with a flick of the wipers.

"Remember and never forget," echoed from the silhouette, loud enough so all the animals of Walla Wunga Forest could hear. "Never lose faith, my friends. Always and forever, believe in the magic of love."

The silhouette faded into the blue skies. Shelby turned to thank Nia, but she was gone as well. Shelby placed her paw over her heart. Though Nia was no longer present, she knew her spirit would always be with her.

Ricky lifted his paw and tapped Theodore on the back. "Thank you, Theodore. We couldn't have saved Ranger Mike without you."

"Anytime, my friend!" Theodore replied. He then addressed all the animals of the forest. "I owe everyone an apology," he said. "Never again will I act like a bully. I will work hard every day to make it up to you, all of you."

"That's my boy," said his mom, wiping away the tears.

All the animals joined in: "FRIENDS TOGETHER, FRIENDS FOREVER!" They shouted.

The laughter and all the excitement came to a screeching halt. Wetherbee floated from the sky and landed on an old tree stump right in front of everyone. "Uh-oh," said Bart. "Wetherbee is on the grump again?" The forest was so quiet, you could hear a pine needle drop.

Wetherbee was wearing the meanest snarl the animals had ever seen. He looked to the left and then to the right, up and down and all around. "Sunshine? Warm air?" He grunted. "Well, I have only two words for all of you." The animals cringed, expecting the worst. "LET'S PARTY!" He shouted and wiggled his feathery behind.

"YEAH!" The animals all roared.

Merlin took out his wooden guitar and gathered together the songbirds. "From the sun, to the flowers and trees, oh what a wonderful life," they sang. "We are truly living a dream."

The animals followed Wetherbee's lead and rocked the forest floor.

Ranger Shaun glanced over his shoulder, "That had to be the fastest-moving storm I've ever experienced. One second there are tornadoes everywhere and the next second blue skies. Mother Nature is quite amazing," he said.

Outside of wiping the gnats from the windshield, Ranger Shaun was oblivious to what was going on around him. The attacking vulture dragons, the silhouette, and even the prism of light had escaped his vision.

"How are you, Mike?"

"Twisted my leg pretty bad," Mike replied, "but all in all, I'm okay."

"Well, let's get you to the hospital to have it looked at."

"Hey, do me a favor and circle back to the open field. There was a lot of lightning. I just want to make sure there are no fires."

"Will do," Ranger Shaun said.

Shelby noticed the helicopter returning. "Hey, everyone, gather around!" She yelled out.

Ranger Mike grabbed the door latch and pulled himself up so he could look out the window.

"See anything?" Shaun asked.

The animals had formed a giant heart in the open field. Ranger Mike paused. "Nothing," he replied as a tear trickled from his eye. "Nothing at all."

"Okay," Ranger Shaun said. Ranger Mike smiled gently as they rose up above the treetops. "Thanks, guys," he whispered. "Your secrets will always be safe with me."

THE END

Made in the USA
Middletown, DE
20 December 2018